Published by Scholastic Inc., *Publishers since 1920*, 557 Broadway, New York, NY 10012. SCHOLASTIC and associated logos are trademarks and/or registered trademarks of Scholastic Inc.

Library of Congress Cataloging-in-Publication Data available

ISBN 978-1-338-15941-7

Text by Thea Stilton
Original title *Il segreto delle Fate dei Fiori*
Cover by Caterina Giorgetti (design) and Flavio Ferron (color)
Illustrations by Giuseppe Facciotto (layout), Chiara Balleello and Barbara Pellizzari (pencils and inks), and Alessandro Muscillo (color)
Graphics by Marta Lorini

Special thanks to Tracey West
Translated by Emily Clement
Interior design by Becky James

10 9 8 7 6 5 4 3 2 1 17 18 19 20 21

Printed in China 38

First edition, October 2017

Geronimo Stilton

Thea Stilton
THE LAND OF FLOWERS

Scholastic Inc.

Thea Stilton and the Thea Sisters
THEA
PAULINA
Colette
Violet
Nicky
PAMELA

WELCOME TO THE LAND OF FLOWERS, THE KINGDOM OF THE FLOWER FAIRIES! COME MEET THE BEAUTIFUL AND MYSTERIOUS CREATURES WHO LIVE IN THIS COLORFUL WORLD . . .

Dewdrop Fairies are tiny fairies with shining wings. They live on the Green Petal Plain and sprinkle dewdrops over the flowers every morning.

Yarrow the elf is the royal gardener. He wears a special pendant, which is the key to the Timeless Rose Garden, the most mysterious place in the kingdom!

Flora and Farrah are princesses. These twins love their kingdom and would do anything to protect it. They live at Golden Dahlia Palace with the Fairies of the Four Seasons.

Butterfly Fairies are kind, peaceful fairies with large butterfly wings. They live in a small village where they tend to flowers and prepare special healing potions.

Melania is the Queen Bee Fairy of Honeyville. Bee Fairies are careful, hardworking creatures, and they produce the best and most nutritious honey in the whole kingdom.

The Fairy of Good Counsel is a solitary creature who lives at the center of the Hawthorn Labyrinth. She guards the Golden Flowers: precious blooms that can only be picked by those who demonstrate wisdom, intelligence, and love.

Helios is a Knight of the Order of the Sunflower. Loyal and brave, he is searching for his beloved Farrah, who has mysteriously disappeared.

Green Sprites are tiny creatures who live in the trees. They love to cook and hold a contest every year to find the greatest chef in the kingdom.

Perfume Fairies are kind creatures who live in the enchanted town of Happy Blossom, where they distill the most fragrant flower petals to collect their sweet-smelling scents.

THERE'S A SCENT IN THE AIR . . .

Violet ran down the halls of Mouseford Academy. She had exciting news to tell her friends — the four other mouselets known as the Thea Sisters.

"Look what I found!" she cried as she ran into Colette and Pam's room.

"What is it?" asked Paulina.

"It's the flyer for the academy's Spring Festival!" Violet answered.

"Is it spring already?" Pam asked. "My fur is still frozen from winter!"

Violet's eyes shone with excitement. "This is my favorite time of year. I love this festival!"

"What does the flyer say?" asked Pam.

"The festival needs **VOLUNTEERS** to work on different committees," Violet explained.

Pam spoke up first. "I'll help with the **food**! We can have cheese pizza, and cheese balls, and cheese dip . . ."

"I can think of some **games** we can all play together outside," Nicky added.

Then Colette entered the room. Her blonde hair was rolled in big, **pink curlers**.

"What's going on?" she asked.

"What have you got on your head?!" Nicky asked, giggling.

"It's a way to get wavy curls without ruining your hair," Colette replied. "One of my favorite beauty bloggers put up a video showing how to do it."

"It looks like you're wearing a **HAIR HELMET**," Pam teased.

Colette laughed. "You still haven't answered my question," she reminded her friends.

Violet showed her the flyer. "It's almost time for the Spring Festival."

"Ooh, yes!" Colette cheered. "I have some great ideas for decorations this year. Who wants to be on the committee with me?"

"I'd **love** to," Violet said.

"Me, too," added Paulina. "Do you already have some ideas?"

Nicky spoke up. "I've been thinking that the theme should be SPRING FLOWERS."

"That's perfect!" said Colette. "We could create beautiful DISPLAYS of fresh flowers."

"And we could make colorful paper butterflies and **dragonflies** to go with the displays," Paulina suggested.

"These are all great ideas for the festival," Colette agreed. "I'll be right back. Time to take out the curlers!"

Just then, a messenger knocked on the half-open door.

"A PACKAGE for Violet," he said.

"Who's it from?" Nicky wanted to know.

"It's from CHINA," Violet said. "My parents sent it."

"Come on, don't keep us in **SUSPENSE**.

Show us what's inside!" cried Pam.

Violet opened the package and took out a BOOK with flowers on the cover. "My mom knew I was excited about the Spring Festival, and I asked her to send me some **inspiration**," she said.

Paulina looked over her shoulder. "These *illustrations* are beautiful!"

Colette walked back in the room. Nicky gasped.

"**COCO, YOUR HAIR LOOKS AMAZING!**" she cried.

The other Thea Sisters agreed.

Colette patted one of her soft curls. "What did I tell you?" She smiled. "**Guaranteed** results!"

Then her eyes fell on Violet's book. "What

pretty floral arrangements!" she exclaimed. "I know. Let's head to the Dolphin Club and start working on our ideas. Then we can bring them to the festival committees."

"GREAT!" said Nicky. "We could make some sample flower arrangements."

"Can we make one for Thea, too?" Pam asked.

"That's a great idea!" cried Paulina.

Thea Stilton was a journalist, an adventurer, a teacher at Mouseford Academy — and the reason the friends called themselves the THEA SISTERS. She had called on Paulina, Nicky, Pam, Colette, and Violet several times to accompany her on missions for the TOP SECRET Seven Roses Unit.

"We can leave it on her desk so that she'll

find it when she gets back from her journalism conference," Paulina said. "It will be the perfect way to say . . .

WELCOME BACK TO MOUSEFORD!"

A CALL FOR HELP

The friends quickly gathered supplies and headed to the Dolphin Club, ready to get to work on their ideas.

"I'll work on the buffet menu," Pam immediately offered. "I brought a snack with me so I won't get too hungry."

"I'll help you," said Paulina.

"And I'll make a list of games," added Nicky.

"Great, then Colette and I will focus on decorations," said Violet as she flipped through the pages of her book with Colette.

"**This is gorgeous!**" she exclaimed, pointing to a picture of a vase holding PURPLE flowers.

I'll plan the menu!
I'll do games!
And we'll do decorations!

"Violet flowers for Violet," Colette teased. "Of course! But where will we find flowers like these?"

Violet smiled. "It's wisteria, a climbing plant native to China," she said. She held up a piece of purple paper. "But we can make some pretty bouquets out of paper."

They picked up the scissors and got busy. Colette WATCHED what Violet was doing.

"Your flowers are so Pretty," she said. She held up the flowers she was cutting. "Mine are looking wilted."

"It's okay. You just need to fluff them up a little. See?" Violet said.

She skillfully touched them, and they soon looked perfect.

"FANTASTIC!" Colette said.

While they continued to make flowers, Pam and Paulina were discussing the menu.

Pam said. "So, I like the idea of cheese sandwiches cut into flower shapes."

"Definitely! And we could place them on a bed of lettuce, so they look like they're in a field," Paulina suggested enthusiastically.

Pam nodded. "Awesome. What about dessert? Flower-shaped cookies?"

"Or how about cupcakes decorated with SPRING COLORS?" Paulina asked.

Paulina started typing into her tablet. "Let me look up some recipes."

Violet approached them, holding a small bouquet of purple paper flowers. "What do you think?" she asked.

"Wow, they look SO REAL!" Nicky said.

"These are wisteria," Violet explained. "The real one is a very thick vine that grows around tree trunks."

Colette held up her bouquet. "And making the flowers out of paper is perfect because they will last until Thea gets back from her conference."

"Let's go put them in her office now!" Pam suggested.

They walked through the halls of the academy until they arrived at Thea's office. The door was unlocked, and the room was EMPTY and silent.

Then they heard something . . .

Some kind of music seemed to be coming from far away.

"Maybe it's the ringtone of a cell phone," Pamela guessed, looking around.

Colette pointed to a BLUE BOX

on Thea's desk. "It's coming from here," she said.

"Should we **answer** it?" asked Violet.

"Let's at least see who it is . . . it could be something **important**," said Pam, opening the lid.

Right away, the Thea Sisters recognized the **super-secret cell phone**. It had been given to Thea by Will Mystery, the head of the Seven Roses Unit.

"Will only calls Thea on this phone when there's an **EMERGENCY**," said Violet.

Paulina looked worried. "Oh no. I have a **bad feeling** about this call!"

THE SEVEN ROSES UNIT

The headquarters of the Seven Roses Unit is hidden in icy Antarctica. Only the members of the unit know how to find the entrance.

WILL MYSTERY

He is the director of the Seven Roses Unit, a super-secret research center that studies fantasy worlds inhabited by characters from fables and legends.

The Hall of the Seven Roses

In the heart of the unit is the Hall of the Seven Roses. It is a living map that shows every Fantasy World and reports each one's condition. When a world is in danger, a crack appears in the map. Next to the map is a crystal elevator that travels to the fantasy worlds. Only Will Mystery can make it work.

The Thea Sisters

The Thea Sisters became agents of the Seven Roses Unit thanks to their great investigative abilities. They work in secret and help the unit whenever they are called.

The Rose Pendant

Each researcher has a pendant that contains their personal information. It can be used as a key to open doors in the unit headquarters.

A NEW SECRET MISSION

"What do we do?" asked Colette.

"We know it's **Will Mystery**," Paulina replied. "We should pick up."

"We shouldn't **answer**," said Violet. "It's Thea's phone."

"We could start a **video chat** with Thea and ask her," Pam suggested.

"Great idea! I'll connect us now," said Paulina, typing on her **TABLET**.

Thea's response came right away. "Mouselets! How are you?"

"We're good, but something important has come up," Paulina said. "The **super-secret cell phone** that Will gave you is ringing. Should we answer?"

"Of course! Right away!"

Pam pushed a button on the phone, and the face of the director of the **SEVEN ROSES UNIT** appeared on the screen.

"Hello, Will!" she greeted him.

Will looked surprised. "Pam?"

Pam then explained, "We're on a **video chat** with Thea, who's at a conference. Give me a sec to get a **secure connection**, and I'll add your call to Paulina's tablet."

Pam **quickly** set up the call. Will didn't wait to get to the point.

"Everyone, unfortunately I have **BAD NEWS**," he began.

"Oh no!"' they all cried.

Will continued, "I called you because something of the **greatest urgency** has happened. Thea, can you and the Thea Sisters come see me?"

Her response wasn't what Will was expecting. "I'm sorry, Will, but I'm at a journalism conference, and I'm one of the speakers. If I leave suddenly, it might be difficult to keep the unit's secret. But I'm sure my students can help you."

"Of course we will!" Paulina said.

"Excellent," said Will. "I'll send the **ultrasonic helicopter** to the beach at Mouseford Academy at exactly nine o'clock

tonight. There's no time to waste."

"*We'll be there!*" the Thea Sisters replied.

"One more thing," Will continued. "The helicopter is silent, so you won't hear it approach. Look for a **BLINKING LIGHT** that resembles a shooting star."

"**Cool!**" Paulina commented.

Will smiled. "See you soon."

Then his face disappeared from the tablet's DISPLAY.

"Thank you for taking on the CHALLENGE, mouselets," Thea told them. "You've faced many difficult missions already. By now you're all experts."

"It won't be the same without you, though . . ." Violet said.

Thea nodded. "I'll try to join you if I can," she promised. "But you all should go and get ready. It will be DARK soon."

"We'll stay in touch, Thea," Paulina said.

"I have faith in you, never forget that," Thea said. "And now that you five are SPECIAL AGENTS, I'm sure you'll be able to do this without me."

"It's strange leaving without you. But **we won't let you down**," Nicky assured her.

They ended the call and returned to their rooms to get **ready**. A few hours later, they walked through the **garden** to the Mouseford beach, carefully and silently . . .

A STRANGE WELCOME

The **helicopter** arrived on the beach at exactly nine p.m. It looked just like a **shooting star** falling from the sky, as Will had said. The Thea Sisters quickly boarded it, and it flew away from Whale Island without anyone else noticing.

Their **adventure** had begun!

"I'm a little **nervous** this time. Maybe because Thea isn't with us," Violet admitted.

"It'll be fine, Vi. And we'll get back in plenty of time for the **Spring Festival**," Colette promised.

Even Nicky, who was usually so **confident**, sounded anxious. "Do you really think we can do it?" she asked. "We

have no idea what's waiting for us."

"Will always knows what to do," Paulina reminded them.

"Oh yeah . . . Will is so BRAVE and strong . . ." Pamela teased her.

Paulina blushed. She had a little crush on Will Mystery, and her friends all knew it.

The helicopter flew at incredible speed to Antarctica. It hovered at the hidden entrance and then descended under the ice to the landing pad.

The Thea Sisters got out. Nobody was there to greet them. The helicopter quickly took off again.

"How strange. Usually Will is here to meet us," Colette commented.

"He said this was a very SERIOUS mission,"

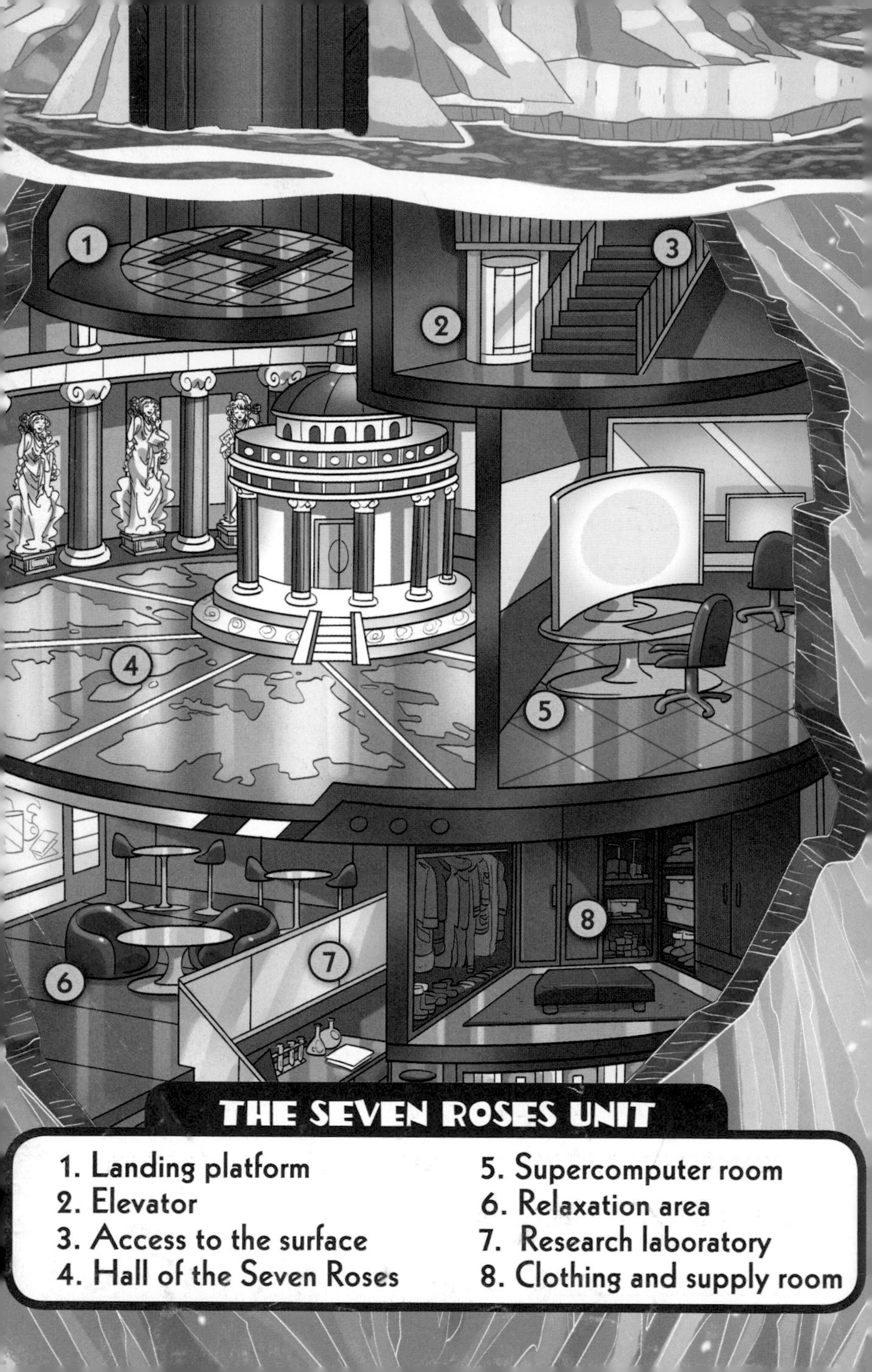

THE SEVEN ROSES UNIT

1. Landing platform
2. Elevator
3. Access to the surface
4. Hall of the Seven Roses
5. Supercomputer room
6. Relaxation area
7. Research laboratory
8. Clothing and supply room

Nicky said. "He's probably too busy."

"Let's go look for him in the **HALL OF THE SEVEN ROSES**," Pam suggested.

"Good idea!" the others agreed.

They had been to the SECRET HEADQUARTERS of the unit several times before, and they knew their way around.

They walked down a long, silent hallway. When they arrived at the **HALL OF THE SEVEN ROSES**, they found it deserted.

"Will's not here," Pamela said, looking around. "The whole place is too **quiet**. This is getting weird."

Paulina took a few steps into the room. The floor and ceiling were covered with maps: **living maps** that showed each of the fantasy worlds. The maps **changed** whenever something happened to change one of the fantasy worlds.

Where's Will?
The maps are all blurry!
Look!

Paulina looked at the maps and gasped. "The maps are all **blurry**!"

"You're right," said Violet. "It's as though a **dark cloud** is covering them all."

"There is **something wrong** with all of the maps," Nicky agreed. "That's **NEVER** happened before!"

Paulina nodded. "It's true. Usually a **CRACK** appears in a map when the world is in danger. But this is really different."

"Now they must **ALL BE IN DANGER** at once!" said Colette.

The Thea Sisters suddenly understood why Will was so busy.

This would be their **most challenging** mission yet!

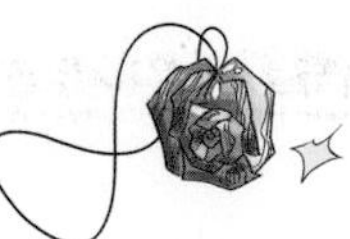

WILL'S SECRET

The Thea Sisters were still looking at the **living maps** when they heard a voice behind them.

"**Welcome**, Thea Sisters. I knew I'd find you here."

They turned to see **Will Mystery**, the director of the Seven Roses Unit.

"**WILL!**" the five friends cried.

"I'm sorry I couldn't greet you when you arrived," he said. "I've been **BURIED** in research. The fantasy worlds are in **big trouble**."

"What can we do to **HELP** them?" Paulina asked.

"I'm working on that," Will explained. "But I can't explain it to you here. Follow me."

"You're acting very mysterious today, Will," Nicky commented as they left the Seven Roses Unit.

"You're right, Nicky. But there's a reason for that." He stopped and looked at them intently. "I'm about to bring you all inside the **heart** of the Seven Roses Unit. Only one other agent besides me has access to it."

"And you're bringing **US** there?" Paulina asked.

Will nodded. "You all have proven that you are skilled agents — and absolutely trustworthy. You have been to many of the fantasy lands and helped save them. That's why I asked you to **HELP** with this mission."

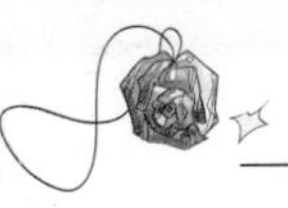

"Wow!" exclaimed Pam. "So I guess now we're, like, **super-secret** agents."

"Exactly," he replied.

"**We won't let you down, Will,**" Colette said confidently.

They all put their paws together.

"**We're stronger together!**" cried Nicky.

Will nodded. "Now come with me. Time is running out!"

The Thea Sisters followed Will out of the Hall of Seven Roses and down another hallway. Will was quiet and the girls decided not to ask him other questions yet.

At the end of the hallway, Will stopped in front of a metal door. He moved his eyes in front of a sensor that made a BEEP of recognition. Then he took his crystal PENDANT and inserted it into a slot. There was another BEEP.

Finally, Will placed his paw on a digital pawprint reader. They heard one final BEEP, and the

Security Level 2 2

metal door slid open.

"Wow, talk about **SECURITY**!" Pam exclaimed.

"It's necessary," Will said, and motioned for the others to step inside.

They found themselves inside a GLASS tube.

"It's an ELEVATOR," Paulina remarked.

"With no buttons," added Nicky.

"The computer responds to the sound of my voice," Will said. Then he spoke loudly. **"LEVEL ZERO."**

The elevator door closed, and it began to **rise**.

"Shouldn't Level Zero be at the Bottom of the headquarters?" Paulina asked.

Will smiled. "You'll understand when we get there."

THE SANCTUARY OF THE SEVEN ROSES

The elevator reached its destination. "This is the place where it all began," Will told them. "It's where the unit gets its **name**."

The Thea Sisters gazed around at the circular room. **Flowery** wallpaper decorated the walls. And in the center was a display case with a **glass bubble** containing seven roses, each in a different **COLOR**.

"These are the **SEVEN ROSES**," Will told them.

The five friends all gasped.

"**They're beautiful!**" Colette exclaimed.

"You should have seen them the day they arrived here. They **shone** with an amazing

Here are the Seven Roses!
Wow!

LIGHT," he replied. "But now . . . they seem to be dying."

"Why are these roses so **important**, Will?" Colette wanted to know.

Just then, a rodent with blonde hair and GLASSES walked toward them.

"Hi, Linda," Will greeted her.

She gave him a smile and then turned to the mouselets.

"You must be the Thea Sisters. **Welcome!**" she said.

"Linda is our expert botanist. She takes care of the Seven Roses," Will explained.

Colette smiled. "It's nice to meet you, Linda," she said.

"I'm **happy** to meet all of you," Linda replied. "Will has told me all about you and your

work on earlier **MISSIONS**. I hope that you can help us this time, too."

Will took a **CLOSER LOOK** at the Seven Roses. "Is there any **news**?" he asked.

Linda shook her head. "Unfortunately not. The situation is the same as it was yesterday, and I'm afraid it will get **worse**."

"What does it mean that the roses are **dying**?" Paulina asked.

"We should first explain the **history** of these roses," Linda replied, with a glance at Will. "You see, these roses are special because we brought them here from one of the **FANTASY** worlds: the Land of Flowers."

"**LAND OF FLOWERS?**" Pam repeated.

Linda nodded. "Flowers of every kind grow there. And it's inhabited by the Flower Fairies. They're very sweet and lovely creatures."

Colette gasped. "If the roses are dying, then the Land of Flowers must be in trouble!"

"Exactly, Colette," said Will.

Linda motioned them over to the DISPLAY CASE containing the roses.

"These roses are special," she explained. "They don't have THORNS. They never stop blooming, and they radiate PURE LIGHT. But now their petals are wilting."

She showed them a PHOTO. "They used

to look like this," she explained.

"The flowers are linked to the health of the **LAND OF FLOWERS**," Will added. "But they are also linked to the Seven Roses Unit."

"It's because of these **SEVEN ROSES** that the unit can communicate with the fantasy worlds," Linda explained. "But now that they're **DYING** . . ."

"The whole unit is in **JEOPARDY**!" Colette realized.

"That must be why the maps in the Hall of Seven Roses are cloudy," Paulina guessed.

Will nodded. "Exactly. The roses are our LINK to the fantasy worlds."

Nicky gasped. "And if they die, then the Seven Roses Unit will lose contact with the fantasy worlds!"

"Holey cheese! We need to **do something**, fast!" Pam cried.

"There's only one thing to do: We must go to the **LAND OF FLOWERS** and find out what's happening before it's **TOO LATE**," Will concluded. "If we don't, we will lose our connection to these amazing worlds forever!"

THE LAND OF FLOWERS

"So how do we save the **roses**?" Violet asked.

"I am not sure," Will said. "But I believe we will find the answer in the **LAND OF FLOWERS**. As usual, I'll need to brief you about where we're going."

Linda handed him a **BOOK**.

The Land of Flowers . . .

"The Land of Flowers was the first **FANTASY WORLD** that I explored," Will began. "I spent a lot of time in that **enchanted land** and learned much about it, and the **flower fairies** who live there."

Will opened the book. "While I

was there, the Flower Fairies gave me this book," he said. "It contains watercolor paintings of their world."

Violet, the artist of the group, leaned in for a closer look.

"How beautiful," she said, looking at a picture of an enormouse Golden Flower.

"This is Golden Dahlia Palace," Will said. "Believe me, it's even more beautiful in person."

"Who lives in the palace?" Paulina asked.

"Before I tell you that, you need to know more about the kingdom," Will answered. "The palace is the heart of the Land of Flowers, surrounded by blooms of every size, shape, and color."

"It must smell wonderful!" cried Colette.

"The scent of flowers is everywhere," Will said. "They're all different, but they

work together in wonderful harmony."

The mouselets smiled at the thought.

Will continued, "The Flower Fairies are very kind and pleasant creatures, as delicate as the flowers they take care of."

He turned the page to a painting of a fairy wearing a gown made of BLUE

flower petals. "Here is one of them."

"What a gorgeous dress!" Colette exclaimed. "Do you think the fairies would be willing to give us some fashion ideas for the Spring Festival?"

Nicky nudged her. "Colette! This is a real emergency, not a fashion emergency," she reminded her.

"Oh, right! I forgot," Colette replied.

Will continued his briefing. "The fairy court lives at the palace. It is divided into the Spring Flower Fairies, the Summer Flower Fairies, the Autumn Flower Fairies, and the Winter Flower Fairies. As you can imagine, the fairies in each group are EXPERTS in the flowers of their season."

"Will, do the flowers all grow wild, or are there

gardens at the palace?" Violet asked.

"There is a large and beautiful garden there," Will said.

"Is there a snack bar?" Pam asked.

"No, but the palace and garden are protected by a moat made up of flowers," Will replied. "These are special flowers — the Flowers of Forgetfulness. Anyone who smells them will become confused and lose their sense of direction."

"Wow! That's a good defense! Who thought of that?" Pamela asked, curious.

"Yarrow, the royal gardener. Here's his portrait," Will said, turning the page.

"What's that strange PENDANT he's wearing around his neck?" Nicky asked.

"It's the **first flower** that ever grew in the

kingdom," Will replied. "The pendant is also the key to the Eternal Rose Garden, where the Seven Roses once grew."

Paulina got a gleam in her eye. "That's where we'll learn why the roses here are dying!"

Will nodded. "Yes, but only Yarrow and the princesses can take us there."

"Princesses? How many?" Paulina asked.

Will turned another page and stopped at a portrait.

"Two. They're TWIN SISTERS," Will explained. "They look identical, but their personalities are as different as NIGHT and day."

"She looks sweet," said Colette, pointing to a fairy in a pale peach dress.

"That is Flora," said Will. "She's usually cheerful and happy. Her sister, Farrah, can be mysterious and moody. That's her in

the BLUE dress."

"They're different — just like the five of us," Pam remarked.

Paulina smiled. "Yes. But that's what makes our friendship so strong!"

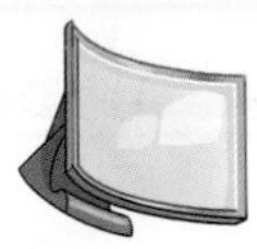

DESTINATION: LAND OF FLOWERS!

The Thea Sisters flipped through the pages of the album, drawn in by Will's tale.

"I'm sorry to **interrupt**, but we must continue the briefing," Will said. "I've programmed the **supercomputer** for a complete report on the Land of Flowers. It should be finished by now."

Violet looked at the Seven Roses in the display case. "I hope the *flowers* don't die before we can figure out what's wrong."

Linda held up a bottle of **green** liquid. "I've been working on a new **natural fertilizer**," she said. "I think it can help keep their condition from getting worse — for a little while, anyway."

Will placed his paw on Linda's shoulder. "**Thanks**, Linda. Do what you can to keep them alive."

"And we'll **do our best** to find out what's wrong," Paulina promised.

The Thea Sisters said good-bye to Linda and left the secret room with Will. They took the elevator to the room containing the most **POWERFUL COMPUTER** in the Seven Roses Unit.

On every **MISSION**, the supercomputer had provided them with helpful information.

Will approached the keyboard and typed in "**LAND OF FLOWERS**," and then hit ENTER.

A few seconds later, **PICTURES** and **captions** appeared on the screen.

"There's so much information here," Paulina said, scrolling through the pages. "Where should we start?"

"I can give you ten minutes," Will replied. "*Scan* it as best you can. There are countless *flowers* and **creatures** in this fantasy world, and you won't be able to remember them all."

The Thea Sisters huddled together and began to read about the Land of Flowers.

While they read, Will filled a **backpack** with supplies.

"I'll take a few useful things," he told them. "A flashlight, some *rope*, a **COMPASS** . . ."

Nicky noticed Will packing a small jar. "What's that?"

THE LAND OF FLOWERS

BLUE BEETLES

These insects look like large blue ladybugs. They watch over Golden Dahlia Palace.

ABILITIES: Their long antennae that can detect small movements. They can fly quickly over long distances using their strong wings.

EQUIPMENT: They carry sharp spears to discourage intruders.

THE COAT OF ARMS

The coat of arms shows the first dahlia that grew in the kingdom. The yellow flower was sculpted in gold and surrounded by diamonds that look like dewdrops. The original is kept in a crystal case in the princesses' rooms, while a copy is located at the entrance to the palace.

THE GREAT BOOK OF FLOWERS

Yarrow, the royal gardener, takes care of this precious book. It contains everything known about the kingdom's flowers. Over the centuries, royal gardeners have added new plants, pictures, and information to the book.

"It's a special flower essence," he answered. "I can't open it here, because we may need it later."

"Ooh, so mysterious," said Colette.

"You'll find out more about it, trust me," Will assured her. Then, growing serious, he added, "It's already daylight in the Land of Flowers, so we must go."

The Thea Sisters followed him toward the CRYSTAL ELEVATOR.

When they were all inside, Will typed on the keyboard and beautiful music filled the elevator. Colorful light swirled all around them.

Then the light faded, the music ended, and the elevator doors opened. The Thea Sisters and Will stepped out onto a blossoming field that extended as far as they could see. A light, perfumed breeze caressed their faces.

"This is such a pretty shade of GREEN," Paulina remarked.

"And look at the YELLOW sky!" Nicky added.

Violet knelt down. "This is very unusual-looking grass."

"Actually, it's not grass," Will said. "Take a closer look."

Violet did just that.

Wow!
Beautiful!

It's the Land of Flowers!

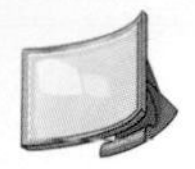

"You're right! These are green flowers. **Amazing!**"

"These flowers give this place its name: It's called the Green Petal Plain," Will explained.

"That's perfect!" Pam commented.

"Do any fairies live on this plain?" asked Paulina.

"If I remember correctly, we should find the Dewdrop Fairies here," he replied.

Pam looked around. "I don't see any fairies."

"They're very small and shy," Will explained. "But

their wings sparkle in the sunlight."

Violet saw something SHIMMERING in one of the flowers close by.

"I think I see one!" she exclaimed.

A graceful fairy flew up from the flower. She wore a white dress, and pale blue wings fluttered on her back. She held a gold wand topped with a star.

"That's a DEWDROP WAND," Will explained. "Every day, the fairies fly over this wonderful field and WATER them with dewdrops."

As he spoke, the rays of the sun suddenly became

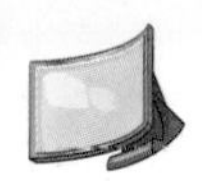

very **BRIGHT**. All around them the petals, damp with dew, *reflected* the rays of light.

"We need to cross this **plain** to get to the palace," Will instructed.

"The **LIGHT** is too strong here. I can't **SEE** anything," said Nicky, shading her eyes with one paw.

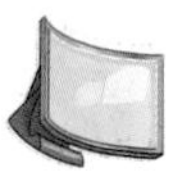

"Try to **follow me**," Will said as he moved forward, his face turned toward the ground.

The researcher found a narrow path among the flowers and followed it.

"We should have brought **sunglasses**!" Pam exclaimed.

"They wouldn't help a bit!" Will replied. "No sunglasses could ever shade you from

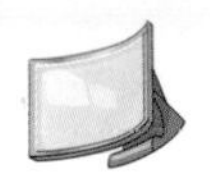

the brilliant light of the Kingdom of Flowers. Keep your eyes on the feet of the mouselet in front of you so that you won't get lost," Will suggested.

The Thea Sisters tried that, and it worked!

"**Thanks, Will!**" the girls cried, and followed him.

A short way away, though, they all noticed something strange.

Look!

"Will, all of the flowers here have withered," said Colette.

Will stopped and LOOKED at the flowers.

"You're right," he said. "This means the situation is even **more serious** than I thought."

"Why have the flowers withered?" asked Violet.

"For the same reason

the Seven Roses have wilted: Some danger is THREATENING this world!" Will replied. "We must find out what it is."

"Right! And to do that, we need to get to the *palace*," said Nicky.

"How will we ever get there if we can't SEE where we're going?" Colette wondered.

The friends kept going, when suddenly they all heard a **sound**.

It was a *light rustling*, like the fluttering of wings . . .

"Is someone **following** us?" Pam called out.

THE DEWDROP FAIRIES

"Maybe they've lost their way," whispered a voice behind the Thea Sisters.

They all turned around and saw two fairies suspended in midair, watching them timidly.

"Actually, we need your help, kind fairies," Will replied.

"How could we be of any HELP?" one of them asked.

"We would like to reach Golden Dahlia Palace, but it's very difficult to cross this plain," he replied.

"The light is too bright," Violet explained.

The fairies exchanged a look. Then one of them replied, "WE'LL GLADLY HELP YOU!"

She pulled out a long, transparent thread that shone in the sunlight.

"Am I seeing things, or is that thread made of pure light?" Pam asked.

"It's thread made of enchanted dew, woven with moonlight," replied the second fairy. "It's very **strong**, in spite of its appearance."

Two more Dewdrop Fairies flew up to join them.

"What's going on?" they asked.

"We're helping these travelers cross the plain," one of the fairies explained.

The two new fairies

agreed to **help**. The fairy holding the thread handed one end of it to Will.

"Hold the thread tightly and **follow me**," she instructed. "Don't let go."

Will passed the thread down to the **THEA SISTERS**. Each one held it in her paw.

"Let's walk in single file," he suggested. "Just be **careful** not to drop the dewdrop thread."

The girls formed a **LINE**.

"Is everyone ready?" one of the fairies asked.

"READY!" they responded.

Then the Dewdrop Fairies flew ahead of them, guiding them through the plain.

Soon the group crossed into another part of the plain where even more of the green flowers had wilted.

Pam discovered this first. "Look, the flowers have withered here, too!" she announced.

"Unfortunately this isn't the only place," one of the fairies said sadly. "We have seen MANY withered flowers in our beloved Green Petal Plain."

"Why is this happening to the flowers?" asked Colette.

"The heat of the sun is becoming more intense, and it is drying out the soil," she replied. "And the wind crosses the plain with STRONG GUSTS that rip out our seedlings."

"This has **never happened** before," another fairy added. "We're not sure what's causing it."

"We **WATER** the plain every day with our dew wands, but it's not enough," said the fourth fairy.

"That's exactly why we're heading to the ***Golden Dahlia Palace***," Will explained. "We're going to find answers."

"Let us hurry, then," said one of the fairies, fluttering her wings.

THERE WAS NO TIME TO WASTE!

BEYOND THE RAINBOW FREESIA

"We're here. This is the end of the Green Petal Plain," announced one of the fairies.

The girls returned the dewdrop thread to the fairies and looked around. Now that they were beyond the plain, the sunlight was not as bright.

"Thank you so much for your help," said Violet.

"Without you we would never have been able to cross the plain," Paulina added.

"It was truly a pleasure to help you," one of the fairies replied. "We hope that you can bring **harmony** back to the Land of Flowers.

"Take the path beyond the Rainbow Freesia

Clearing, and then go over the **MOUNTAINS**." the fairy instructed.

Colette **GAZED** at the horizon. "What strange mountains! They look **PURPLE**!"

"Those are the **VIOLET PEAKS**," one of the fairies replied with a smile.

"They're beautiful," Violet said, smiling.

"Yes, but WATCH OUT: You must be very careful while passing through them," said a third fairy.

"The violets can TRICK you," another fairy explained. "They can sense travelers passing through them and set them on the wrong path."

Nicky's eyes got wide. "I've climbed MOUNTAINS all over Australia, but never one with flowers that can trick you!" she remarked.

"We'll be careful," Will promised. "Thanks again for your help."

The Dewdrop Fairies waved good-bye and then flew away, back over the green plain.

Will started to walk. "Let's get to the VIOLET PEAKS!" he said, and the Thea Sisters followed him.

"Did you CROSS them the last time you

came here?" Nicky wanted to know.

"No, never," he replied. "When I visited this kingdom the first time, I used a secret passage and followed a different path."

Paulina looked surprised. "You didn't use the crystal elevator?"

"No, that didn't exist yet," Will replied. "I created that a few years later. I was a very young, inexperienced researcher when I made my first trip here."

The group continued walking in the direction of the Violet Peaks and soon reached a clearing full of flowers in many colors: white, purple, yellow, orange, red, and blue.

"These are the Rainbow Freesia that the Dewdrop Fairies were talking about!" cried Violet, sniffing the air.

"Wonderful," said Paulina. "I wish we

weren't in such a hurry. I could stay here for days."

"This world is so full of colors and wonderful smells, we can't let it disappear!" Colette exclaimed.

Will and the Thea Sisters left the *freesia clearing* behind them and continued. The landscape now led gently toward the mountains. They sloped up toward the sky, covered in a blanket of purple flowers.

Violet gasped. "I've never seen so many violets in one place," she said.

"Yes, these MOUNTAINS are clearly meant for you, Vi," Colette observed affectionately.

Nicky scanned the mountain peaks. "There's a path over there that goes up the slope," she said, pointing.

"Let's take it," Will said. "But remember the fairy's warning. The flowers will sense us and may try to redirect us."

Pam looked up at the mountains. "We have to climb all the way up there?"

"It shouldn't be too hard," Nicky promised. "Come on!"

They started climbing confidently. But Violet and Colette hung back.

"This is a pretty steep slope," Colette said. "And we're not even sure

Beautiful!
Oooh!
Look!

What a view!

if this is the right path."

"Any of these paths could get us over the mountains," Will replied. "We just have to move carefully, and try not to be **fooled**. I have faith in all of you."

"Okay. **LET'S GO!**" Colette cried.

Then she and Violet followed Will and the others up the mountain of violets.

THE VIOLET PEAKS

They made their way up, up, up the mountainside. The path got STEEPER with each step they took.

"STAY STRONG, everyone!" Will called out in encouragement. "We're about halfway there."

But the HIGHER they climbed, the stranger things became. The blanket of violets would ***shift*** suddenly, sending them in a different direction. They were ZIGZAGGING up the peak, but not getting anywhere.

"This is a LOSING battle," Pam said, panting.

"It seems like we'll **never** get to the top!" Colette agreed.

Nicky spoke up. "The **fairies** warned us about this. Just keep **calm**, and take it one step at a time. We'll make it."

But they went a

little bit farther and discovered that the path ended abruptly. Will stopped at the edge and frowned.

"It's a **DEAD END**, we can't pass through here. We must turn back," he said, discouraged. But just as he said it, the path moved again. It curved, leading back up the mountain!

"**Quick**, follow it, before it changes direction again!" Pam cried, and everyone ***rushed*** to stay on the path.

Colette shook her head. "It's as if the mountain is joking with us."

"Or maybe it doesn't want us to cross it," Paulina remarked.

"That's not possible. **MOUNTAINS** don't **WANT** things," Pam objected.

"This one does," said Will. "And we must find a way to figure out its **TRICKS**, or

we'll **NEVER** get to the palace."

Pam frowned, thinking. "There must be another way through these mountains."

"**Yes!**" cried Nicky. "I bet that's the answer. If every path keeps **changing**, maybe we're not supposed to take a path at all."

Pam shook her curls. "Okay, now I'm really confused."

Excited, Nicky walked over to a ROCKY WALL. She **sniffed** the air and ran her paws through the purple violets. The others watched her curiously for a moment. Suddenly, her face brightened.

Come look!

"I think I **FOUND** something!" she announced. "There's something back there," said Nicky.

Will took a look. "You're right. That looks like a **tunnel** carved into the rock."

"How did you find it?" Colette asked Nicky.

"There's a different smell here, beneath

the smell of the flowers," Nicky explained. "A **DARK**, **underground** smell."

Will took a **FLASHLIGHT** out of his backpack. He moved aside the curtain of violets covering the entrance to the tunnel.

Will stepped into the **tunnel**, and the Thea Sisters followed him.

"Step carefully," Will warned. "Let's see where this goes."

Their heads almost touched the STONE ceiling above them as they slowly made their way through the mountain.

"Will this tunnel ever end?" Pam wondered after they had walked for a long time.

"If it gets us to the other side of the mountains, like I think it does, then it may take a while," Nicky replied.

They walked on, with only Will's FLASHLIGHT to guide them. A few minutes later, a dim light appeared in the distance.

THE MYSTERIOUS CAVE

"That must be the **EXIT**!" cried Pamela. "Finally! I was starting to feel **TRAPPED**."

Will frowned. "We haven't gone ***very far*** yet," he said. "I don't think it's the way out."

"Then what is it?" Paulina asked.

They walked closer, and their questions were answered. The passage opened into a beautiful **PURPLE** cave. Amethyst crystals grew from the cave floor, and purple **stalactites** hung from the roof like icicles.

"This place . . . It's incredible," said Violet, looking around, amazed.

"I didn't even know this cave existed," Will said.

Wow!
Listen!
It's a song!

mmmm mmmm mmmm mmmm
mmmm mmmm mmmm mmmm
mmmm mmmm mmmm mmmm
mmmm
It's coming from here!

Then a strange melody floated into the cave, coming from the distance.

"It sounds like someone is singing!" Colette exclaimed.

"Let's go see," suggested Will, and he headed toward the sound. "Maybe it's someone who can point us in the right direction."

They followed Will, and, a short distance away, between two purple rocks, they saw two fairies, kneeling.

As soon as the fairies noticed the visitors, they stopped singing and turned toward them.

"Excuse me, we don't want to disturb you," Will began.

They didn't respond.

"Maybe they don't understand what we're saying," Colette guessed.

Then one of the fairies stood up, not taking her eyes off them.

Nicky took a step forward. “Hello, kind fairies,” she said. “We are headed to Golden Dahlia Palace. Could you guide us to the SHORTEST path to get there?”

Only then did the fairy speak, in an airy voice. “You say you are going to the palace?”

“The Land of Flowers is in DANGER,” explained Will. “We must reach the palace as soon as possible.”

“We do not know anything about the world outside,” the fairy replied. “We can never leave this cave.”

“Why can’t you leave?” asked Colette.

“We are the Fairies of the Ghost Flowers,” she explained. “They grow here in the DARKNESS of the cave, with no light. We WATCH OVER them.”

The Ghost Flowers . . .

"Thank you anyway, kind fairies," Will said. He turned to walk away — but he found he couldn't take a single step! **Large roots** were winding around his legs.

"**HELP!**" he shouted. "I can't move!"

Pam turned to the fairies. "**Let him go, please!**"

"It's not our fault," replied the fairy, sounding **sorry**.

Then more **roots** sprang from the ground and **GRABBED** Pam's leg.

More roots sprang up, wrapping around the legs of the other Thea Sisters before they could run.

"**STOP THIS!**" Nicky demanded.

"I'm sorry," the other fairy replied. "But we can't **help** you. It is the **Ghost Flowers**. Whenever visitors pass this way, the flowers try to hold on to them."

"We have nothing to do with it," said the first fairy. "We are only their guardians."

"We have never even **SEEN** the rest of the Land of Flowers," the other said. "The Ghost Flowers take pity on us."

Will suddenly had an idea. "Paulina, take out the ALBUM that's in my backpack and give it to the fairies."

She rummaged around and took out the

book they had LEAFED through before leaving the Seven Roses Unit.

"What is this?" asked the first fairy, taking it from Paulina's paws.

"YOUR WORLD," replied Will. "There are pictures of all the things you've never seen."

"Really?" the second fairy asked. Then they both started to turn the pages. Soon, they were smiling. "This is amazing! Look at all the beautiful places."

"You may keep the book," Will said, "in exchange for helping us find a path through these mountains."

The fairies looked at each other. Suddenly, the roots retreated back into the ground.

"WE'RE FREE!" cried Pam.

"And now we will keep our end of the bargain," one of the fairies said. "Go straight

through the cave. Beyond the AMETHYST QUARTZ ARCH you will find a passageway that will take you outside the Violet Peaks."

Will and the Thea Sisters said good-bye to the fairies.

"That album of the **LAND OF FLOWERS** was very precious," Paulina said. "It must have been **difficult** to leave it behind."

"I have an idea," Violet said. "We'll **draw** a new one together when this is all over!"

"Good idea, but this **adventure** is far from over," Will said.

Then they all walked out of the cave.

THE BLOOMING STREAM

The Thea Sisters and Will Mystery walked until they reached the AMETHYST QUARTZ ARCH that the fairies had told them about. It was carved with MYSTERIOUS symbols and led to a NARROW PASSAGE carved into the rock.

"It looks **spooky** in there," Colette said with a shiver.

"We've got no choice," Nicky said. "Besides, I don't think those fairies would send us into DANGER."

Oooh . . .
We have to go in there?

They entered the **DARK** passage and continued to make their way through the mountain.

"It's weird," Colette remarked after a while. "It's so humid in here. My curls are getting completely flat!"

"Don't worry, Colette, you're still gorgeous!" Pam teased her.

They walked on in silence. Once again, Will's flashlight was the only thing that lit the way. After a few minutes, they all heard a shout.

"HEEEEEEEEEEELP!"

It was Pam's voice! Will spun around, shining the FLASHLIGHT in her direction. There was no Pam — only a **GAP** in

the rocky path that all the others had missed.

"**PAM!**" Violet cried. "She was right behind me a second ago. What could have happened?"

"Could she have fallen through that crack in the ground?" Paulina asked.

"She must have," said Nicky. "Where **else** would she go?"

She knelt by the gap and peered down. "It's really **DARK** down there. We've got to go after her!"

"You're right, Nicky," Will agreed. "Let me get a better **LOOK**."

He cautiously moved toward the crack in the ground and shone his flashlight through the gap.

"*Listen!*" he called out. "I hear running **WATER**."

Will pointed the **FLASHLIGHT** toward the sound. "It's an

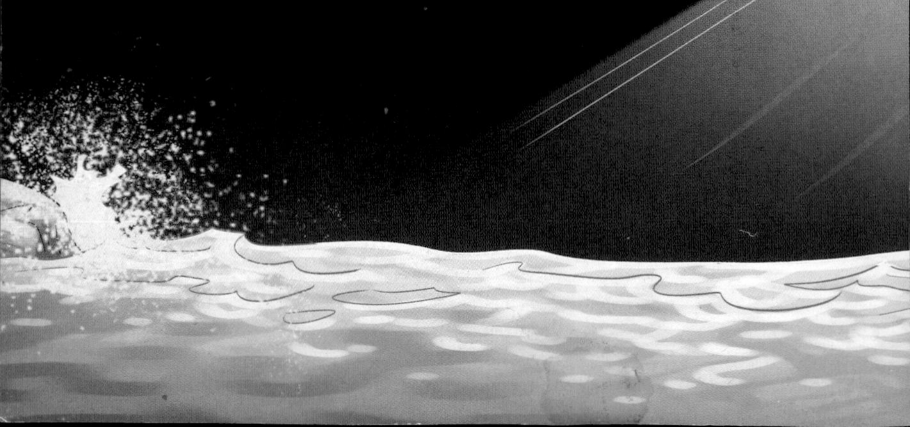

underground **stream**," he replied.

"Could Pam have fallen into the **WATER**?" Paulina asked.

"It's possible," Will replied.

"The ***current*** is very strong. It must have carried her away."

"**POOR PAM!**" Violet exclaimed. "I hope she's okay."

"We have to go after her, but it will be **DANGEROUS**," Will said. "I trust you are all **strong** swimmers?"

"Yes!" replied Nicky, and the others nodded in agreement.

"Good," said Will. "We'll jump into the water and follow the **current** to find Pam."

Will opened his backpack and took out a rope. Then he tied one end of the rope around a rock to **ANCHOR** it.

"I'll go first," Nicky offered.

Violet looked down into the crack. "I'm frightened to jump down there," she admitted.

"I am, too," Colette said. "But we've got to do it for Pam!"

Nicky grabbed the end of the rope and dropped down through the crack. They

heard a splash as she entered the water.

"It's cold!" she called back up as the water carried her away.

Colette and then Paulina **carefully** slid down the rope into the water. Then it was Violet's turn. She GRIPPED the rope, counted to three, and slid to the bottom.

Inch by inch she descended until she felt the water beneath her feet.

"Now let go!" Will encouraged her from above.

Violet nodded. "We're coming, Pam!" she cried, and then she dropped into the water with a splash.

Will sealed his WATERPROOF backpack, slid down the rope, and dropped into the water after her.

THE LILY FROGS

Right away, Will noticed that the water smelled like flowers. As the current gently pulled him forward, he shone his flashlight ahead. He couldn't see any of the Thea Sisters.

Before he had time to worry, Will felt something moving under him. He looked down to see a large frog beneath him! The frog had an unusual collar around its neck that looked like flower **petals**. Even more unusual was the fact that the frog was giving him a ride!

The frog brought Will to the place where the river opened into a marvelous underground lake dotted with **water lilies**.

There, Will saw all of the Thea Sisters — even Pam! They were also riding those strange frogs.

"Pam! Are you okay?" Will asked.

Pam nodded. "Just a little soggy."

"These **kind** creatures brought us here," Colette explained.

Then one of the frogs spoke. "We are the

Lily Frogs. We're happy to help you!"

"And they said that the **way out** of the Violet Peaks is close by," added Paulina.

Another frog chimed in. "We'll take you there now, but we must **go quickly**!"

"Why?" Pam asked. "Can't we **EXPLORE** this lake first?"

"There is no time to **explain**," the frog replied. "You must trust us!"

"**Hold on tight!**" said another frog.

The frogs **swam** until they reached the river. Soon Will and the Thea Sisters could see a **BRIGHT LIGHT** ahead.

When they reached the light, they saw an

opening in the rocks. Nicky realized something.

"**THAT'S A WATERFALL!**" she cried.

One by one, the **Lily Frogs** jumped forward, carried by the waterfall, and fell safely into the deep, crystal clear water of the lake below.

"You're outside the mountains now!" Will's frog said.

"Wow! That was some **LEAP**!" Paulina told her frog.

Suddenly, the water **stopped** falling from the rocks.

"**Just in time**," said Will's frog.

"If there's no water, then it's not possible to pass through the waterfall," Colette's frog explained.

"But why did the river DRY UP so suddenly?" Nicky asked.

"The water runs at NIGHT and stops when the sun rises," explained the frog.

"Why does it do that?" asked Violet.

"Because when the water stops, the water level of the lake goes down," the frog replied. "That means that the flowers that are usually covered by the water can take in the sunlight. It is perfect harmony, found only here in the LAND OF FLOWERS."

"That is a very beautiful system," Violet said. "Thank you for explaining it to us."

"Before you go, can you please tell us how to get to the Golden Dahlia Palace?" Will asked.

His frog nodded. "Cross the forest that borders the lake and look for Twirling Daffodil Way. But remember this: Only if all the daffodils are turned toward you will they point you in the right direction."

"What if they aren't?" Pam asked.

"Well, then you must earn their trust, but it's not easy to do," the frog replied.

"How do we earn the trust of a daffodil?" asked Colette.

"No one really knows," her frog replied.

The frogs said good-bye and swam away.

"The palace can't be that far now," Will said. "Let's go."

After a short walk, a field of yellow flowers appeared in the distance.

"That must be Twirling Daffodil Way!" Colette cried.

TWIRLING DAFFODIL WAY

The Thea Sisters and Will approached Twirling Daffodil Way, a long field of tall, YELLOW flowers.

"Look! The daffodils are facing in **every** direction," Violet said.

"**OH NO!**" cried Paulina. "That

Hey!

means they won't let us pass!"

"**I'll try anyway,**" said Pam. She took a few steps into the daffodil field.

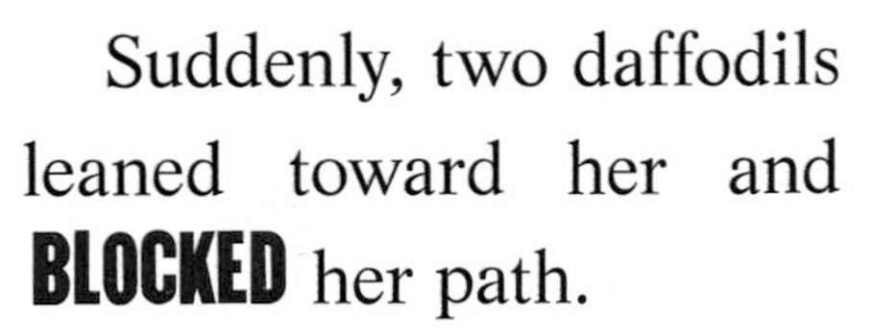

Suddenly, two daffodils leaned toward her and **BLOCKED** her path.

"It looks like the **Lily Frogs** were right," said Will. "The daffodils won't let us ***pass***."

"We have to find a way to **convince** them," added Nicky.

"How are we supposed to do that?" Pam asked.

Will and the others were trying to figure out a solution when

Violet **noticed** something. One of the smaller daffodils had been **uprooted** from the ground.

She walked over to see better. "**OH, YOU POOR THING!**" she cried.

Without hesitating, she quickly knelt down and dug a hole in the earth with her paws. Then she placed the **flower bulb** in the hole and covered it up.

"Will, can I have the canteen of **WATER**, please?" she asked.

Will passed it to her and kept talking with the other Thea Sisters.

Violet watered the newly planted flower. In just a few seconds, the stem straightened up toward the sky and the petals opened in all their splendor.

Then she smiled with satisfaction and returned to her friends.

"Maybe we can talk to them, and they'll listen," Colette was saying.

Then they all turned toward the daffodils. This time, to their great surprise, they saw that all the flowers were facing them! Now they could see that at the center of the golden field was a long path that led off beyond the horizon.

"What happened?" Will asked, surprised.

"I don't know," replied Paulina. "But it seems that the daffodils have decided to help us."

Then they all looked at Violet, realizing

that she hadn't taken part in their discussion before.

"Did you do something, Vi?" Colette asked.

"Oh, no. I just replanted a flower that had fallen over," she replied timidly.

Paulina hugged her tightly. "You're a genius! You've earned the trust of the daffodils!"

"But . . . I didn't do it on purpose," she replied.

"That's why the daffodils have turned toward us now," Colette replied.

Violet blushed and smiled. "Any of you would have done the same."

"Now we should go, before the daffodils think twice and turn away from us again," Will said.

They continued to walk, following the path that had opened up in the field of daffodils,

How beautiful!

which watched over them like **TALL STATUES.**

When they reached the end, they all let out a sigh of relief.

"Whew! I'm glad we got away from those weird flowers," Pam said.

"When we get to the *palace*, we'll see all kinds of flowers," Will said. "We're close. You can already smell the Flowering Moat that surrounds the palace."

"Colette, it smells like the perfume you wear," Pam remarked.

Colette sniffed the air. "I don't know. This smells a lot **stronger** than any perfume I've ever worn."

"It's not just strong, Colette," Will said. "The smell of these flowers can also be **DANGEROUS!**"

CROSSING THE FLOWERING MOAT

"I remember," Paulina said. "The Flowers of Forgetfulness will try to trick us."

"They'll make us lose our sense of direction," Colette added. "We will never reach the palace, and we'll wander the moat forever."

They were all silent for a minute as they gazed out at the Flowering Moat. The enormouse flower bed surrounding the Golden Dahlia Palace contained thousands of flowers with large, colorful petals that gave off a strong fragrance.

"So how do we get through it?" Nicky asked.

"Should we **hold** our snouts?" Pam suggested.

Will shook his head. "No, that won't work," he said. "The essence of these flowers is dangerous even if you breathe it in through your mouth."

"So it's an impossible task!" Pam said.

Then Will reached into his backpack. "Fortunately, it's not. I brought along something that should be useful," he said, showing them a GLASS BOTTLE.

"That's what we saw back at the Seven Roses Unit," Paulina recalled.

Will nodded. "It's dahlia essence, the only fragrance that can lead us through the moat to the palace."

Everyone **breathed in** some of the

precious essence. Then Will took the lead guiding them into the moat. It was a truly wild forest of **multicolored flowers**, with blooms that gave off a strange odor.

The Thea Sisters made their way through the moat, wondering at the beautiful flowers all around them. Violet saw one flower in an unusual shade of orange and moved closer to it to get a better look.

But Violet got **too close**, and the scent of the Flower of Forgetfulness quickly **OVERPOWERED** the dahlia essence. Her eyes glazed over. She started to wander away from the others.

"**VIOLET, NO!**" Colette cried. She grabbed Violet by the paw and led her back to the path.

Colette kept an eye on her friend after that. They walked quickly, and soon the flower moat opened up onto a path that led to a beautiful, golden gate.

"**We're here!**" Will announced.

Two flying **Blue Beetles** hovered in front of the gate. They **GLARED** at the visitors with angry black eyes.

"Will told us about the Blue Beetles," Nicky whispered to Paulina. "They **GUARD** the palace. They won't let just anyone in."

Will stepped toward them. "Hello! I'm Will Mystery, and these are my colleagues. We are here to meet with the princesses, Flora and Farrah."

"**Impossible!**" the two beetles said firmly.

"May I ask why?" Will said politely.

"Princess Farrah has left the palace," replied one beetle.

"And Princess Flora is very sad," said the other.

"**No one may enter!**" they finished.

"But your kingdom is in danger, and we believe we can help you," Will argued. "You must let us in right away."

"**Impossible!**" the two beetles repeated.

Will retreated and huddled with the Thea Sisters. They talked in whispers.

"I don't think they're going to change their minds," Paulina said.

"Isn't there another **ENTRANCE** we could use?" asked Nicky.

Will shook his head and replied. "No, this is the only way in. I'm not sure what we can do if these **beetles** won't let us pass."

Then they heard someone call out behind them. "Will Mystery! Is that you?"

Everyone turned to see a tall elf smiling at them.

"Yarrow!" Will greeted him. "How nice to see a friendly face."

"Come with me, quickly!" the elf said shortly, and they all followed him.

They took a hidden path until they reached another GATE, smaller and made of iron, and mostly covered with ivy. Yarrow stopped in front of the gate and touched the PENDANT he wore around his neck.

Suddenly a STRONG LIGHT burst forth from the pendant and the gate opened with a metallic sound.

"We're about to enter the **Timeless Rose Garden**," the gardener warned them. "I beg you, please do not touch the roses for any reason. It's very dangerous!"

They all nodded, and when they entered the garden, they GASPED in amazement.

Roses of many different kinds grew on BUSHES all around the garden, but they didn't look like any roses they had seen before.

Violet drew close to a rose with petals as dark as night. "This rose looks like it's made of velvet." Violet reached out to feel the petals of the flower.

"Please don't touch them!" Yarrow shouted. "All of these plants are unique species that grow only here. That's why they are so precious," the gardener said.

"The Seven Roses that I brought to the unit are not in good health, Yarrow," Will explained. "That's why we've come here."

Yarrow nodded. "Here, too, the situation is growing hopeless. Some of the roses have

already permanently **wilted**."

"Can the flowers be saved?" asked Nicky.

"I don't know, but we must try," said the elf. "First, it's important for you to learn what has happened at ***Golden Dahlia Palace***."

THE STORY OF THE TWO SISTERS

Will and the Thea Sisters sat down on two benches as the gardener elf told his tale.

Yarrow began his story. "Harmony and **happiness** have always reigned in the Land of Flowers. Then one day, **PRINCESS FARRAH** fled the palace with a wicked stranger."

"She ran away?" Paulina asked.

Then one day . . .

"Yes, and she has NOT returned," Yarrow said. "But it gets worse. Before fleeing, the princess stole some of the **Mother Roses** from the Timeless Rose Garden."

"Why would the princess do something like that?" asked Colette.

"According to an ANCIENT legend, by distilling the precious essence of the Mother Roses of the Timeless Rose Garden, one can obtain the **Absolute Elixir**," Will answered. "It's a MAGIC POTION that gives the power to control the Land of Flowers."

"So you think the stranger who fled with her convinced Farrah to **steal** the Mother Roses to conquer the Land of Flowers?" asked Pam.

"It seems so, yes," Yarrow answered.

"Why didn't he **steal** them himself?" asked Nicky.

"Because only the **princesses** and I can touch the roses," Yarrow replied.

"That **jasmine** plant was once a fairy. She touched the roses and was instantly transformed into a plant. That is why I asked you to be **careful** and not touch anything when you entered."

"We'll keep our **paws** to ourselves, promise!" Pam assured him.

"Don't you have any idea where Princess Farrah might be?" asked Nicky.

Yarrow nodded. "We believe that the **stranger** took her to a mysterious place at the edge of the kingdom, where the **Tower of the Dark Tulip** is located."

"Dark, dangerous forces lurk in that tower, but we don't know much about them," the elf admitted. "Many have journeyed into those **shadowy lands**, but no one has ever returned."

"What about Princess Flora?" Will wanted to know.

"She shut herself up in her rooms, alone with her **grief**," Yarrow replied. "All she does is cry. And, along with her, the kingdom is slowly losing its bloom."

"Why? Tell us more," said Paulina.

"Because of the THEFT of the roses, the Timeless Rose Garden is **wilting** and with it the entire kingdom, which receives nutrients from the roots of the **Mother Roses**," he explained.

"Of course, it's all connected!" Will exclaimed. "That's why the roses in the Seven Roses Unit are withering, too!"

Yarrow nodded. "Yes, Will. If we don't find a way to replant the stolen roses in the rose garden, soon the LAND OF FLOWERS will die."

"Then we have to find PRINCESS FARRAH," Will said.

"It's too DANGEROUS!" Yarrow protested.

"It doesn't matter. We must do it," Will replied. "But first, we should see Princess Flora."

Yarrow sighed. "Follow me, then."

The elf led them into the entrance of Golden Dahlia Palace.

As the Thea Sisters crossed over the threshold, their jaws dropped.

Welcome!

Here we are!
What a wonderful smell!

PRINCESS FLORA

"This is the Hall of the Flower Fairies," Will explained as they walked into the palace. "I remember spending many hours here with the fairies of the court, watching them sing, make flower crowns, and read poetry."

"It's a very beautiful room," said Paulina. "But I only see a few fairies here now. Where are the others?"

Will frowned. "Things have changed. The last time I came to the palace, the atmosphere was joyful and peaceful. But now . . ."

". . . now we're here, and we're going to save the Land of Flowers!" cried Pam confidently. "We'll find Farrah and bring the roses back to the Timeless Rose Garden!"

Then they heard a voice as sweet as a song. "Do you really think you can save my kingdom?"

"Princess Flora!" Will greeted her, bowing deeply.

"Will, Yarrow, I am so **happy** you both are here," she replied, walking up to them.

Then she looked into his eyes. "The kingdom is in grave DANGER," she said, "but somehow I knew that you would come back and help us."

"I'm sorry I didn't get here faster. But I brought with me some of the BEST AGENTS in the Seven Roses Unit," Will explained. "These are the Thea Sisters."

All five bowed their heads to the princess, and she nodded to them.

"It's an HONOR to have you as guests in my kingdom, kind friends, and I thank you for anything you can do for us," she said.

"Princess, we'll do our best to find your sister and bring back the stolen roses," Colette assured her.

At these words, Flora began to cry.

"Forgive me," said Flora. "It's just that any time I think of my sister, I get so sad. It's as

if a part of me disappeared along with her."

Paulina nodded. "If anything happened to my sister, I'd be heartbroken, too."

Flora nodded. "But now you are all here, and I am grateful. You can stay here with Yarrow and keep WATCH over the palace and the Timeless Rose Garden. I will search for my sister."

"I will stay here and protect the palace," Will assured her. "The Thea Sisters will go with you."

The princess threw her arms around Will's neck and hugged him.

"Thank you SO MUCH, Will," she said, and then she walked away.

Nicky turned to Will. "Do you think we have enough experience for this mission?"

"Of course. I have great faith in all of you," he replied.

"We won't disappoint you," the Thea Sisters promised.

Will's words had filled the hearts of the five friends with pride and courage.

"Let me take you to the throne room," Will said, and they followed him there. RED, PINK, and BLUE orchids were draped around the room's tall, white columns.

A short while later, Princess Flora rejoined them in the throne room.

"Do you have any ideas about the stranger who FLED with Farrah?" asked Colette.

The princess nodded. "There's a rumor about a young man who once belonged to

the **Knights of the Sunflower**, an ancient, noble order, which has always been a credit to this kingdom. This is their **coat of**

arms," she said, pointing to an elegant tapestry behind her. It showed three sunflowers entwined around two crossed SWORDS.

"So this knight left the order?" Will asked.

"He disappeared mysteriously, after he was accused of practicing magic," Princess Flora replied. "MAGIC has always been banned from the Land of Flowers."

"How did your sister meet this knight?" Colette asked.

"One day, my sister ventured to the western part of the kingdom," Princess Flora answered. "That's where the Lilies of False Memory grow. They are beautiful white flowers, but they are dangerous. They can confuse your memories."

"Farrah smelled the lilies and then lost her way home," the princess continued. "The

knight found her wandering and brought her back to the palace."

"That doesn't sound WICKED. That sounds kind," Nicky remarked.

"Yes, but the knight remained at the palace. Two days later, the roses were stolen and Farrah disappeared," Princess Flora explained. "That night, she was seen with a mysterious, HOODED figure. And we never saw the knight again, either."

"So you suspect that the knight convinced Farrah to steal the roses for him?" Pam asked.

Princess Flora nodded. "Sadly, that is exactly what I think happened."

THE CRYSTAL COMPASS

After Princess Flora told her story, Will spoke up. "Yarrow told us about the **TOWER OF THE DARK TULIP**. Do you suspect that the knight might have taken Princess Farrah there?"

The princess nodded. "Yes, some travelers reported that they saw my sister and the hooded figure venturing into those **DARK LANDS**."

"I don't understand, why would they go there?" asked Nicky.

"Since the dawn of time, many knights have tried to travel to that tower to take possession of the **Scepter of the Dark Tulip**," Flora said. "It is a scepter with an

onyX tulip set into the top. It is very powerful."

"More powerful than the Absolute Elixir?" Will asked.

"The elixir cannot be used without the scepter," Princess Flora replied. "But the scepter is guarded by a WITCH named Amarantha."

The princess walked away and returned a moment later with a small BOOK with a dark cover. She opened it to a page showing a picture. "This is the scepter. If this knight is taking my sister to the TOWER OF THE DARK TULIP, they must be going after it. I'm sure he plans to take over the whole kingdom."

"Do you think this guy has your sister under some kind of **dark spell**?" Pam asked.

"That is the only explanation," Princess Flora replied. "I know my sister. Someone — or something — confused her and caused her to fall under an enchantment."

"We've got to go to the tower," Paulina said.

Princess Flora frowned. "It's a **DANGEROUS** place and the way there is not clear. All I really know is that we must head north — and that it won't be an easy journey."

Nicky smiled. "Journeys are never easy on our missions."

"We will take the **Crystal Compass** with us," Princess Flora said. "It always points **north**, so it will help

keep us on the right path."

"I'm guessing that the WITCH might try to confuse us with her magic as we get closer to the tower, right?" Paulina asked.

The princess nodded. "Exactly. We must be prepared for her to try to stop us."

The princess handed Colette a small velvet box, shaped like a flower.

"I will leave the compass with you while I gather the fairies together to announce our departure," she said.

Then Flora shook the silver bracelet on her wrist three times, making a sweet jingling noise.

"The fairies will be here soon," she announced.

In fact, the Fairies of the Four Seasons began to arrive in the throne room almost immediately.

When they had all gathered, Princess Flora spoke to them.

"My dear fairies, allow me to present our new friends, the Thea Sisters," she began. "They have arrived from very far away to help us bring Farrah home. I called you all here to tell you that I will be leaving with them to travel to the Tower of the Dark Tulip, where I hope to find my beloved sister. Will Mystery, whom you already know, will stay here at the palace with Yarrow. They will protect the Timeless Rose Garden, and all of you."

The fairies in the hall began to whisper to one another. Then a Winter Flower Fairy spoke up.

"Princess, you're all we have left. Please, be careful," she pleaded. "The tower is a very dangerous place."

"Don't worry about me," Princess Flora replied. "I am confident that, together, the Thea Sisters and I will bring Princess Farrah home **safe** and sound, and will return **harmony** to our kingdom."

The fairies **CHEERED** Princess Flora and the mouselets. It was time for the mission to begin!

WATCH OUT FOR THE NETTLE GRASS!

The Thea Sisters and the princess said goodbye to Will and began their JOURNEY. Soon, the Golden Dahlia Palace was just barely visible in the distance, like a **gigantic golden flower** that watched over the kingdom.

The sun shone on the Land of Flowers as they walked along a pretty green path. Many of the flowers they passed were in **bloom** — but not all. Some were GRAY and drooping.

"The kingdom is suffering," Princess Flora reflected. "And I have stayed shut up in my palace for too long, lost in **sadness** instead of trying to find a solution . . ."

"Of course you were sad," said Violet kindly.

"And now we're taking action, and together we can save the kingdom," Paulina said.

The princess smiled at her. "**Thank you**. You all give me hope."

She stopped to consult the **compass**.

"We must continue this way," she said. Then she flapped her wings and flew to the top of a small hill.

"It would be a lot easier if we could **fly**, too," Colette said, following the princess.

Beyond the hill was a field of long green grass that waved in the breeze.

"It's so pretty!" Violet said.

"It is pretty, but dangerous," the princess explained. "It is called Nettle Grass. Its blades hide a stinging substance that is released when you touch it."

"So how do we cross the valley?" Paulina asked, looking around.

Princess Flora peered into the distance. "There is a land bridge up ahead. It's almost invisible because it blends in with the trees."

When the Thea Sisters reached the bridge, Flora explained, "Hold on **TIGHT** to the vines

That's the Nettle Grass!
We have to cross the bridge!

and don't look down. I'll be flying overhead."

"**I'll go first,**" Pam offered.

She grabbed two thick vines and pulled on them to make sure they would hold. Then she looked back at the others, **COUNTED** to three, and took the first step, holding on tightly.

Flora flew after her until she had reached the other side.

"**Good job!**" her friends called out from the other side.

Next it was Colette's turn. She looked down for just a moment, then took a **deep breath** and continued. She, too, arrived safely. Then it was Violet's turn, and she grabbed the vines **confidently**, having watched her friends. But before she could reach the other side, she stumbled and lost her grip, **falling** off the bridge into the tall grass!

"HELLLPPP!"

Violet shouted, landing in the Nettle Grass.

"Oh no! Violet!" the others cried.

"We have to help her!" Nicky said.

Princess Flora flew above the area where Violet had fallen, but there was very little she could do. She knew that if she got too close to the Nettle Grass, her delicate wings would be damaged.

"She's there in the middle of the grass. I **SEE** her, but I can't reach her!" the princess shouted.

Pam and Colette bravely jumped off the bridge, into the grass.

"OW!" Colette yelped as the sharp grass touched her fur.

"We can't move, or we'll get sliced up like a CHEESE PIZZA!" Pam said.

Nicky and Paulina walked onto the bridge. They reached down and pulled Pam and Colette back up.

"We've got to find another way to help Violet," Nicky said. "If we go down there, we'll only be in trouble, too."

"But why isn't Violet answering us?" Colette asked.

"I am not sure," Princess Flora replied. "And it worries me."

At that moment, they heard the fluttering of wings behind them.

BUTTERFLY FAIRIES TO THE RESCUE!

Everyone turned to see a small group of fairies flying toward them. Princess Flora immediately recognized them. "Butterfly Fairies! I'm so happy to see you!"

"At your service, Princess Flora," one of them replied, her delicate colorful wings fluttering on her back.

"Our friend has fallen into the Nettle Grass, and we can't get to her," the princess replied.

"Leave it to us! Our WINGS are very strong," the fairy replied, and all of the Butterfy Fairies dove into the grass. Seconds later, they emerged — carrying Violet!

The fairies placed Violet on the bridge.

Her EYES were closed, but she was breathing.

"WHAT HAPPENED TO HER?" Nicky asked the princess.

A fairy with purple wings replied. "It's an effect of the grass. It stings very badly, and when it touches someone, they fall into a deep sleep."

We must take her to our village!

"Can you help her?" Princess Flora asked.

The fairy nodded. "We can try to cure her, but we must take her to our village. We have healing potions there."

"You are so **kind**. Thank you!" said Colette.

"It is our duty," the Butterfly Fairy said, smiling. Then she and another fairy placed Violet in a sling made of **BLUE** fabric.

The two fairies took off, **flying**. Then the other Butterfly Fairies **fluttered** around the Thea Sisters.

"Take our hands," said a fairy. "We will take you to our village."

Before they could answer, the fairies grabbed them by the paws and LIFTED them

up. They flew across the land, admiring the magnificent view below.

"We're flying!" Pam cheered.

"It's amazing, but I'm still worried about Violet," Nicky said.

"She'll be better soon," Princess Flora assured her. "Have faith."

As they flew over the Land of Flowers, Nicky, Colette, Pam, and Paulina saw amazing sights. They saw flowers as BIG as trees, in every COLOR imaginable. But here and there they saw spots of gray, wilted flowers.

Princess Flora flew next to them, wearing a concerned look on her face.

"In our village, too, some of the plants are sick, Princess," one of the Butterfly Fairies whispered, guessing her ruler's thoughts.

"I am sorry to hear that," Princess Flora

Fantastic!
We need help!
So many colors!

said. "But I have new hope that things will get better soon."

The fairy smiled at her. "Thank you, Princess. You have given us all new hope."

When they reached the vicinity of their colorful village, the Butterfly Fairies set Violet down on a **bed of flower petals** and called on the fairy most skilled with herbs and medicines.

A fairy dressed in red arrived, carrying a steaming teacup. "This tea is made of the leaves of the Sun Balm flower. It should make her wake up," she explained.

The fairy administered a few sips to the still-sleeping Violet.

"Is it working?" Nicky asked.

The fairy shook her head. "It might not

have been strong enough."

"**What do we do now?**" asked Colette.

"We must take her to **Honeyville**, quickly!" the fairy replied. "There, the Bee Fairies can cure your friend with **Lemon Leaf Honey**," said the fairy.

"Are you sure?" asked Paulina.

The fairy nodded. "Not long ago, a young man who had fallen into the Nettle Grass was brought to them and was cured and recovered."

Flora and the Thea Sisters looked at one another. They were all thinking the same thing: *What if this young man was the* **MYSTERIOUS KNIGHT** *who had left with Farrah?*

"Let's go, then," said the princess. "There's no time to waste!"

We're in Honeyville!

THE SECRET OF HONEYVILLE

Honeyville was closer than the Thea Sisters expected, which was a **good** thing for Violet. They flew there **quickly**, and Princess Flora introduced herself to the inhabitants.

"Good day, fairy worker **bees**. I am Princess **Flora** and I need your help."

The Bee Fairies bowed to her. "Welcome, Princess!" they said as one.

Pam sniffed the air.

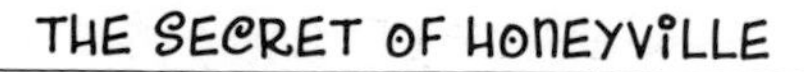

"Something smells sweet and yummy!"

"It's our delicious honey," one of the fairies responded proudly.

"How can we help you?" asked the Bee Fairy, turning to the new arrivals.

"Our friend Violet fell into the Nettle Grass," the princess explained.

One of the Bee Fairies flew over to Violet. "You did well to bring her to us," she said. "Wait for me here."

She rushed off, BUZZING, and returned shortly with a little wooden cask and a heart-shaped leaf. Then she knelt down, dipped the leaf in the cask, and delicately spread honey over Violet's forehead and arms. Then she waited.

After a few seconds, Violet moved her head and slowly opened her EYES.

Colette ran to hug her. "Vi!"

"How do you feel?" asked the Bee Fairy.

"My head is spinning, but I'm okay. Where am I?" she asked while trying to sit up.

"Stay still. It's better if you rest for a little while," Princess Flora advised her.

Violet looked around curiously. "But . . . where am I?" she asked again.

"Lots of things have happened, Vi, since you fell in the Nettle Grass," Colette began.

"The Butterfly Fairies rescued you and brought you to their village to be **cured**," Princess Flora explained. "But their POTION wasn't strong enough, so they brought you here, to **Honeyville**. The Bee Fairies have saved you."

"I don't know how to thank you," Violet said to the Bee Fairy in front of her.

"I'm happy to have helped you," she said.

"Can you tell me if you recently cured a young man who had fallen into the grass?" Princess Flora asked.

"Actually, yes," the Bee Fairy said. "How did you know?"

"A **Knight of the Sunflower**?" Colette asked.

"Was he with someone?" Nicky added.

"And do you know where he was headed?" Paulina asked.

"To tell the truth, he's still here, in Honeyville," the Bee Fairy replied.

Princess Flora's eyes shone with hope. "Can we meet him?" she asked.

The Bee Fairy shook her head. "Unfortunately, Princess, that's not possible." She lowered her voice to a whisper. "The knight is a personal guest of the queen of Honeyville."

"Then take me to the queen," Princess Flora said firmly. "I will speak with her."

"As you WISH," replied the Bee Fairy with a deep bow. Then she flew away. Princess Flora followed her, and so did the

Butterfly Fairies, who took the Thea Sisters.

The Bee Fairy flew higher and higher, all the way to a richly decorated balcony.

There, the Bee Fairy stopped and signaled for the rest of the group to follow her inside. They entered a very large room with an impressive golden throne in the middle, where the Queen Bee Fairy was seated.

"Your Majesty, pardon the disturbance," the fairy said, bowing. "These travelers asked to speak with you."

"It's a pleasure to see you again, Queen Melania," Princess Flora said.

"Hello, Your Highness," said the ruler of the bees in a cool voice. "What are you doing here in Honeyville, may I ask?"

"First I wish to thank you," the princess replied. "Your people have helped a friend

who fell victim to the Nettle Grass."

The **Queen Bee Fairy** smiled. "They were pleased to do it. Tell me, is this the reason for your visit?"

"No, Queen Melania. Unfortunately, there's more," Princess Flora replied. "As you must know, the Land of Flowers is in danger. Several **Mother Roses** were stolen from the Timeless Rose Garden, and now the flowers in the kingdom are dying."

"Who could do such a **monstrous** thing?" the queen cried.

"A stranger has tricked my sister, Farrah, and convinced her to steal the flowers."

"That can't be true!" Queen Melania cried.

"Unfortunately, it is," the princess replied. "But I know Farrah's **heart** and I believe that she is under a **DARK SPELL**. We are searching for her and the young man who

She's the Queen Bee Fairy!
Hello, Melania . . .
Your Highness!

tricked her."

"I hope that you can find them both soon, Princess, and bring your sister back to her senses," Queen Melania said.

Colette spoke up. "Excuse me, Queen Melania. A short while ago, a young man was brought here to be healed. A knight."

The queen's eyes narrowed. "And?"

"Was he alone?" Colette continued bravely.

The queen snapped, "It's true, a young knight stopped here, and he was alone."

"May we please meet him?" Pam asked.

"I'm sorry, but that's not possible," Queen Melania replied.

"And why not?" the princess asked.

"The young man is my guest. And he will see no one other than myself," the queen insisted.

Princess Flora stiffened. "Queen Melania, you know that I can **order** you to do this."

"Not this time," the Queen Bee Fairy replied. "You do not command my **heart**, Your Highness. And I will not permit you to take away the knight who has conquered my **heart**."

Flora's eyes widened in **SURPRISE**. "I only want to speak with him."

The **queen** shook her head. "No."

Paulina **whispered** to Princess Flora. "Perhaps we could offer her something

she wants even more than the **love** of this knight . . ."

"That's a good idea," the princess agreed. She turned to the queen again. "Queen Melania, is there something you want in exchange for the chance to meet this young man?"

The queen looked thoughtful. "There *is* something I want."

"What is it?" asked Pam.

Queen Melania hesitated a moment. "I was born queen of the Bee Fairies, and being a good ruler is very important to me," she replied. "I ask you, therefore, to bring me a Golden Flower, a symbol of supreme **wisdom**. If you succeed, I will allow you to speak with the knight."

THE HAWTHORN LABYRINTH

The Bee Fairy who had cured Violet flew to get a bottle of **mint honey** to give to the Thea Sisters for their journey.

Meanwhile, it was time for the Butterfly Fairies to **GO**.

"**Thank you** for all you've done for me!" said Violet to the two who had carried her.

"It was a pleasure to help you. Farewell!" the fairies replied and flew off.

Paulina turned to the group. "Where do we find a Golden Flower?" she asked.

"The Golden Flowers are very **rare**, and they grow in only **one place** in the kingdom," Princess Flora explained.

"Is it **far** from here?" Nicky asked.

"It is not very far, but getting there — and getting the flower — won't be easy," the princess explained. "The flowers grow in a labyrinth and are guarded carefully by the wisest and most caring creature in the kingdom: the **Fairy of Good Counsel**."

"She sounds very nice," Violet said. "Why wouldn't she give us the flower?"

"She is nice," Princess Flora answered. "But she will only give a Golden Flower to those who pass her test."

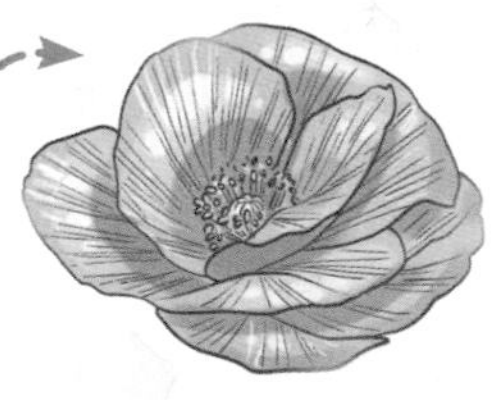

"Is it a math test?" Pam asked. "Because if it is, I'll ace it!"

"I am not sure what kind of questions she asks," the princess admitted. "But they must be **difficult**, because I have not met anyone who has received a Golden Flower

from her."

"But there are **SIX** of us on this mission," Nicky said. "And six heads are better than one! We'll figure it out."

Princess Flora smiled at her. "I can't thank all of you enough," she said. "It means so much to me that you **care** about the Land of Flowers."

She moved away for a moment and returned with six sprigs of **blue flowers**.

"Each of you take one and tie it to your wrist as a sign of my **friendship**. They are Flowers of Sweet Memory. Their perfume has the power to bring back pleasant memories of the one who gave them to you," the princess said.

"This way you'll always remember the

Land of Flowers — and me," Princess Flora explained.

"We could never **forget** you," said Violet.

They left Honeyville and began to walk, following Princess Flora. After a short while, she pointed ahead of them to a large circle made of green bushes.

"There it is. That's the **Hawthorn Labyrinth**," she said

"Princess, have you ever passed through here before? Do you know how to reach the **Fairy of Good Counsel**?" Paulina asked.

"The **labyrinth** is never the same. The hawthorn hedges grow and change constantly," the princess explained. "But if we have faith, the right **path** will open up to us."

Paulina looked confused. "Have faith? What do you mean?"

Can you Get to the House of the Fairy of Good Counsel?

THE HOUSE
OF THE
FAIRY
OF GOOD
COUNSEL

"The Hawthorn Labyrinth isn't a RIDDLE to solve, like other mazes," Princess Flora replied. "There aren't wrong turns or dead ends. We have to pass through it, trusting the labyrinth to guide us. That's the only way to reach the center."

The Thea Sisters weren't sure they understood, but they nodded.

"In any case, be careful, because the leaves of this kind of hawthorn can be very SHARP," Princess Flora warned.

Then she stepped into the labyrinth. On either side of them were tall hedges dotted with white flowers.

"There's such a strong scent in here!" Violet exclaimed.

"Maybe **TOO STRONG**," replied Nicky. "It's making my head spin!"

They walked through the maze. After a few minutes, Paulina stopped.

"Does anyone else have the feeling we're going in circles?" she asked.

"I do," Nicky agreed. "It doesn't feel like we're any closer to the center of the labyrinth."

"Princess Flora has told us all to have faith," Violet reminded them.

"Exactly, Violet," the princess said. "Let go of your fears and trust the labyrinth."

They continued on, following the twisting and turning path. Finally, they saw sunlight at the end of the pathway. They emerged into a round space containing a cute little COTTAGE covered with hawthorn flowers. A fairy in a white dress sat on a bench in front of the house, reading a book. She smiled when she saw them.

"Hello," she said. "I am the Fairy of Good Counsel."

We need your help!

THE FLOWER OF A THOUSAND QUESTIONS

Princess Flora stepped forward. "Kind **Fairy of Good Counsel**, I am so pleased to see you again," she said.

The fairy stood up and bowed. "Princess! Is that really you?"

"We are here because we need to ask you a great favor," the princess replied. "We need a Golden Flower."

The fairy's eyes widened with **SURPRISE**. "May I know why you wish to have a Golden Flower, Your Highness?"

"It is not for me. We need something from Queen Melania, and she has asked for it in exchange," Princess Flora explained.

"An exchange? It must be for something very **important**, if it brought you all the way here. And in the company of strangers," she said, looking at the Thea Sisters with curiosity.

"These are my friends and they are not from this world, but they are here to help me save the Land of Flowers," the princess replied. "I believe that you know what has happened at the Timeless Rose Garden and throughout the Land of Flowers."

The Fairy of Good Counsel nodded. "Certainly, Princess. I know it all."

"Then will you be so kind as to help us?" Princess Flora asked.

The fairy looked thoughtful for a moment.

"Yes, but on one condition," she replied. "Your friends must pick the Golden Flower, without your help."

Princess Flora turned to the Thea Sisters and saw looks of **DETERMINATION** on the face of each one.

"Very well," she responded. "We accept **your condition**."

The fairy went inside the house and returned with a large **daisy** with silver petals.

"This is the *Flower of a Thousand Questions*," she explained. "It's an enchanted flower that never wilts. Each petal contains a riddle that must be solved before you can seek the Golden Flower."

The fairy handed the flower to the Thea Sisters. "Pluck one **petal** to begin," she instructed.

Paulina chose the **first** petal and read aloud the words of a riddle.

They were **quietly** thinking, and then

Three fairies flying high,
Flying high across the sky.
Five flowers down below,
Each one with thirty petals to show.
How many petals much each fairy pick
to pluck each flower clean?

Paulina came out with the answer.

"**Fifty!**"* she said confidently.

The fairy nodded. "Correct. Take a second petal."

This time it was Colette who chose. She pulled off another petal and read the **RIDDLE** out loud.

It lives in the garden, but not in a shack.
This creature carries its house on its back.
Very fast it cannot go,
Instead it moves so very slow.
What is it?

* Paulina used this reasoning: 30 petals multiplied by 5 flowers makes 150 petals. There are 3 fairies, so 150 petals divided among 3 fairies makes 50 petals each!

"I know!" Nicky replied. "It's a snail."

The fairy nodded briskly. "Very good. Now let's see how you do with the third."

This time it was Pamela who took a petal from the flower and read the riddle.

If the fairy Clio is the best friend
of the fairy Luanne,
and the fairy Lucilla is the best friend
of the fairy Odette,
what is the name of the best friend of the fairy Cora?
Muriel, Mira, or Melissa?

Pam frowned. "This one's hard."

"Hold on, Pam," Colette said. "I think we need to look at the **names** of the friends who are paired together."

"You're right, Colette," Violet agreed. "Look at the names Luanne and Clio.

Together, they contain every vowel!"

"So do Odette and Lucilla!" Paulina realized.

Pam nodded her head. "I get it. That means that the best friend of the fairy Cora can only be . . ."

"Muriel!" Colette concluded with a smile. "That is our answer, kind Fairy of Good Counsel."

The fairy smiled back at her. "You have done very well, I must admit."

Then she gave Colette the key that hung around her neck. "This is the key to the gate that protects the field of the Golden Flowers. Take care of it," the fairy instructed.

"Of course," Colette replied.

"Follow me to the gate," the fairy said. "And remember, Golden Flowers are special. Only those who possess a pure

heart, capable of true and sincere **love**, are able to pick them."

When they reached the gate, she gave them five white blindfolds.

"When you enter the field, tie these **blindfolds** over your eyes," she explained. "The purity of your hearts will guide you."

THE GOLDEN FLOWER

The Thea Sisters walked through the GATE and stepped onto the field of YELLOW flowers.

"They're so Pretty!" Violet remarked.

"Why can't we just pick one?" Pam asked. She walked up to a flower and tried to pluck it from the ground. It wouldn't budge. She used two paws, but she couldn't pick the flower.

"**It's impossible!**" Pam cried.

"We should do what the

fairy said," Paulina suggested. "Let's put on our blindfolds."

The Thea Sisters **blindfolded** themselves and started walking slowly through the field, each in a different direction.

"I don't think it's working," Nicky moaned after a little while. "I tried to pick a flower, but the **roots** seemed anchored to the ground."

The other mouselets tried, but even wearing blindfolds, they still were not able to pick the **flowers**.

"What do we do? If we don't bring back at least one to **Queen Melania**, we'll never find Farrah and the missing roses. The Land of Flowers will die!" Violet said.

"Don't give up, Vi!" Pam said. "There's got to be a way to do this."

"I tried **CONCENTRATING** hard, but it's

not working," Paulina said.

"And I tried thinking **good thoughts**, but that didn't work either," Nicky added.

Then, all of a sudden, Colette had an **idea**. "Of course! We have to do it together!"

"What do you mean, Coco?" Nicky asked. "Why would that make a difference?"

"Only those with **pure hearts** capable of love can pick a Golden Flower," Colette replied. "That's what the Fairy of Good Counsel said. It is the **love** we have for one another that makes us strong. **We have to pick the flower together.**"

The Thea Sisters knew Colette was right. They followed the sound of one another's voices and held paws. Then they reached down and grabbed a flower.

"We did it!" Paulina cried. "We picked a **Golden Flower**!"

We did it!

They all untied their blindfolds and couldn't believe their eyes. Paulina proudly held a beautiful Golden Flower.

"This proves that our friendship is STRONGER than anything," Pam remarked. "Together, we can do anything!"

Paulina clutched the flower as the Thea Sisters left the field and returned to the cabin of the Fairy of Good Counsel.

Princess Flora beamed with pride when she saw the Golden Flower in Paulina's paw. "I was sure that there was great love in your hearts," the princess said. "You have done very well. But we must leave here right away, because time is running out."

Colette locked the gate to the field and gave the key back to the Fairy of Good Counsel.

"Thank you," the wise guardian smiled.

"Kind Fairy of Good Counsel, aren't you **SURPRISED** that we managed to *pick* the flower?" Colette asked.

"Princess Flora had **faith** in you, and that is all I needed to know," the fairy replied. "But it is not **difficult** to see the love in your hearts."

"And now, my friend, I have one last **favor** to ask of you," Princess Flora said. "Can you please tell us how to get to the **TOWER OF THE DARK TULIP**?"

The fairy's eyes widened. *"You want to go to the tower, Princess?"*

"We must," Princess Flora replied. "We believe that my sister is being held

prisoner there. We must go there to save her and the kingdom."

The fairy nodded. "I understand, but unfortunately, I can't help you, Princess. I don't know the location of that **dark** and **MYSTERIOUS** tower."

"Can you tell us who would know?" asked Colette hopefully.

"You can ask the Green Sprites," she replied. "It's said that they like to eat a very rare kind of **mushroom** that grows only on the slopes of the mountain where the tower is located."

"How strange!" Nicky said.

"The Green Sprites are **ODD CREATURES**," the fairy admitted. "Be very careful when you meet them: They are kind, but also extremely sensitive and **suspicious**. If they suspect that you want to steal some secret

from them, they will get angry."

"Can you tell us how to get to their village?" the princess asked.

"The village is located in the middle of the Leafy Forest," replied the Fairy of Good Counsel. "When you get there, look for Sweet Moss, a kind of moss that grows on the sides of all the stones there in the north. The sprites can always be found near this moss."

Princess Flora hugged her. "Thank you, kind fairy. You have been of great help to us."

"I am **happy** to help and will be sad to see you go," replied the fairy. "To get out of here, you can pass right through the hawthorn hedge without going back through the whole labyrinth."

"But we'll get hurt!" said Nicky.

The fairy smiled mysteriously. “You’ll be fine, you’ll see.”

Then she said good-bye and disappeared inside her little house.

“Well, let’s give this a try!” Nicky said.

She stepped right up to the GREEN hedge. To everyone’s amazement, the hedge parted right in front of her!

“I guess the fairy was telling the truth,” Pam said.

The hawthorn hedge moved with each STEP they took, and in a short while they were outside the labyrinth. Then the hedge closed behind them.

THE MYSTERIOUS KNIGHT

On the way back to **Honeyville**, Princess Flora turned to the Thea Sisters. "You have all been so wonderful. I want to thank you from the bottom of my **heart** for your help."

"It is a great honor for us to help you," Paulina replied.

Princess Flora smiled and continued, "I know that we come from **different worlds** that are far apart, but I feel that we are becoming true friends!"

"**We are honored, Princess!**" cried Colette, on behalf of all the Thea Sisters.

"Group hug!" yelled Pam, and they all leaned in.

When they reached Honeyville again, they were quickly taken to the **Queen Bee Fairy**.

Queen Melania seemed impatient, pacing back and forth in the throne room.

"Good, you've returned!" she said as soon as she saw the group.

Princess Flora took a few steps forward. "Queen Melania, we have brought you what you asked for."

The queen's eyes lit up with excitement. "Is it true, Your Highness?"

Princess Flora motioned to Violet. She took a step forward and handed the precious Golden Flower to the queen, who brought it up to her face.

"Wonderful! Thanks to this flower I will be able to **protect** my village," the queen said happily.

Pam then voiced the question that everyone wanted to ask. "Can we meet the **young man** now?"

The queen grew serious and called one of the Bee Fairies guarding the throne. "I always keep my promises. Bring our guest here, please."

When the young man entered the room, their suspicions were confirmed.

As soon as the knight saw Princess Flora, his eyes widened with **SURPRISE**. Being twins, she and Princess Farrah looked very much alike.

The princess approached the young stranger and spoke first. "Hello, I am Princess Flora. I see that your coat of arms

belongs to the **Knights of the Sunflower**, the order that stands for courage and nobility of the spirit."

"That is true, Princess," he replied. "My name is **Helios**, and I am a knight of the order."

Princess Flora looked directly into his eyes. "In the name of your order, I ask you to respond honestly to my question: Do you

know my sister, **FARRAH**? Do you know where she is now?"

The young man lowered his **GAZE**. "I do know your sister. But unfortunately, I have no idea where Princess Farrah is now."

"**How can that be?**" Princess Flora asked. "She was last seen leaving the Golden Dahlia Palace with you."

The knight shook his head. "On my honor, that is not true. I met your sister only **twice**. The first time, I found her among the Lilies of False Memory. The princess was wandering, **confused** and afraid, so I helped her and brought her back to ***Golden Dahlia Palace***," Helios explained.

"When was the second time you saw her?" Nicky interjected.

"It was in the palace **GARDEN**," Helios answered. "After our first meeting, I could never forget your sister's face. I gathered my courage and decided to ask her to marry me."

The room fell silent. Colette broke the silence.

"Oh, how romantic!" she cried out.

"It would have been, if only something terrible hadn't happened," Helios said sadly.

"What do you mean?" the princess asked.

"Farrah led me to the Timeless Rose Garden," Helios responded. "It was so beautiful there, but before I could ask her to marry me, a dark, hooded FIGURE appeared between us. The figure cruelly grabbed Farrah's hand from me and struck me. I fell to the ground.

"When I recovered, I saw Farrah following the mysterious figure out of the Timeless Rose Garden," Helios continued.

"It was like she was in some kind of trance."

"Why didn't you chase after them and tackle that hooded creep?" Pam asked.

"I tried to, believe me. But an INVISIBLE FORCE kept me frozen in place," Helios replied. "I believe it was an enchantment, and it took several minutes to wear off. When I could move, I searched for your sister for days and days, until I fell into the Nettle Grass and was then cured by the Bee Fairies."

"Then you have no idea where Farrah is now?" asked Colette.

He shook his head. "She kidnapped her and took her who knows where."

"Wait, 'she'?" Pam asked. "The creep in the hood was a woman? How could you tell?"

"On the day that Farrah disappeared,

the hood slipped back onto the shoulders of the strange figure and I saw her face," Helios went on. "It was wrinkled and **CRUEL**, with sharp purple eyes and an evil sneer. The person who kidnapped your sister was . . . **A WITCH!**"

Hearing the word *witch* jogged Princess Flora's memory. "Yarrow told us about a witch. It must be **Amarantha**, the the evil witch who lives in the Tower of the Dark Tulip!"

IN THE LEAFY FOREST

The Thea Sisters, Princess Flora, and Helios spent the NIGHT in Honeyville, eating a meal of honey cakes and getting a good night's rest.

The next morning, they began their journey to the TOWER OF THE DARK TULIP. They headed to the Leafy Forest to find the Green Sprites as the Fairy of Good Counsel had told them to. Paulina walked next to the knight. "It seems like Queen Melania loved you very much."

Helios nodded. "I am grateful to her.

She cured me when I needed help. But my **heart** belongs to Princess Farrah. I could not give it to the queen."

"She must have understood that, deep down," Colette guessed.

Violet nodded. "That would explain why she made a deal with us for the Golden Flower."

"I am glad that she did," Princess Flora remarked. "Because now we are closer to **FINDING** my sister. Now that I know she is under the spell of an **EVIL WITCH**, I am more worried about her than ever."

"Hey, look, that must be the Leafy Forest," said Nicky, pointing to a cluster of trees in front of them.

"Yes," Helios said. "It's a place of rare beauty, but we must be careful while crossing it."

In silence, the group walked through the thick row of tall trees.

"Start looking for moss on the stones," Helios instructed. "That will help us find the sprites."

Everyone looked down and started looking for traces of Sweet Moss on the rocks in

the undergrowth. They walked **DEEP** into the forest, but they didn't find anything.

"I hope we're headed in the right **direction**," Pam remarked, looking around. "It's easy to get lost in the forest. And we haven't seen any trace of the Sweet Moss . . ."

Just then, Paulina felt something brush against her shoulder. "Hey! What's that?!" she cried.

"It's just a caterpillar," the knight replied. The cute, bright green creature crawled on the back of his hand.

"It's not POISONOUS?" asked Violet.

"There are no poisonous creatures here," the princess replied.

Pam frowned. "Other than the WITCH who kidnapped your sister."

"Hey, I think I found something!" Nicky interrupted her.

She was looking at a BIG ROCK right in front of her.

"We must be certain that it's the right kind of moss," the knight said.

She looked at it carefully, and at last concluded, "Moss of a dark green color, growing on all faces of the rock: It's what we're looking for!"

"The moss will lead us to the village of the sprites," Paulina said.

"HOORAY!" everyone cheered.

So they moved forward, following a line of rocks covered in dark moss on all faces.

"We're getting closer now," Helios said after they had traveled a while. "Let's continue carefully, so we do not alarm the inhabitants of the village."

They proceeded down a gentle slope, and the village of the Green Sprites came into view.

THE VILLAGE OF THE GREEN SPRITES

Pam sniffed the air. "**Something smells delicious!**"

"The sprites are very proud of their cooking," Helios explained, leading them toward the village.

"Excellent," Pam said. "Those honey cakes the Bee Fairies fed us were yummy, but not very filling. I hope the sprites feel like sharing."

But when they reached the bridge leading to the village, they were immediately **BLOCKED** by two sprites. One was perched on a tree branch, and the other was holding a cake. The sprites stared at the visitors curiously.

Who are you?
Hello, kind sprites!
What do you want?

"Who are you, and **WHAT** are you doing here?" asked the sprite in the tree.

Princess Flora smiled. "Pardon the intrusion, kind sprites. I am Princess Flora and these are my friends."

"Princess! It's an honor to welcome you to our village!" said the sprite carrying the cake.

The first sprite frowned. "How do you know that she's really the *princess* if you've never seen her before?"

Helios stepped forward. "I can testify that she is the princess. I am Helios, a Knight of the Order of the Sunflower."

The sprites observed the **coat of arms** on the knight's chest. That seemed to convince them, so they bowed deeply to the princess.

"What is the reason for your visit, Majesty?"

"We're here on an important **MISSION**, and

we need your help," Princess Flora explained.

"We'd like to help, but we're very **busy** here, you know," the sprite replied.

He motioned to the village, where Green Sprites were **scurrying** to and fro, carrying plates of food and cooking pots.

"I understand," the princess said. "Still, if you could please take us to see the **Great Sprite**, I'd be very grateful. We won't take up too much of his time."

The two sprites nodded. "Of course, **follow us**," the sprite replied.

They followed the sprites across the bridge to the **TALLEST** tree in the village. One of the sprites **scrambled** up the trunk and knocked on a door carved into the thick tree.

He went inside the tree, and

returned a few minutes later with another Green Sprite.

"Welcome to our village," he said kindly.

"THANK YOU, GREAT SPRITE!" they all replied.

"What brings you here?" he asked.

"We're on a very important mission, and we need your **help**," Princess Flora replied.

The Great Sprite nodded. "We will give you all the **help** we can, Princess. But you'll have to wait. It's a very special day here in our village."

Colette was curious. "What's happening today?"

The leader of the village smiled proudly. "Today we are awarding the title of . . . Best Cook of the Green Sprites! It's the most important event of the year, and as you can see, the **competition** is about to begin."

"I see, Great Sprite. Then we'll wait until

the competition is over," the princess replied.

"Princess, why don't you ask him to give you the information you need right away?" Paulina whispered to Princess Flora.

"I could, but it wouldn't be right," she whispered back. "The Green Sprites work ALL YEAR to prepare for this festival; asking them to postpone it to help us, even for a very serious reason, would be very RUDE."

"But Farrah could be in DANGER," Helios objected.

"No one knows that better than I, Knight," she told him. "But I am sure that as soon as the competition is over, these kind creatures will help us."

Helios agreed. "As you wish, Princess."

"Excuse me, but how long will the contest last?" Nicky asked.

"Oh, not too long," the sprite replied. "This

year there are only twenty dishes.

"Twenty dishes?!?" Nicky cried.

"We have many great **cooks** in this village, and we let them all compete," the Great Sprite explained.

"Very well, **Great Sprite**," the princess said. "We will wait here."

"Oh, no, Princess!" he cried. "We are so

happy to have you with us today. You and your friends will be the **judges** of our contest this year!"

"We will gladly do it," Princess Flora replied.

As soon as they were seated, the Great Sprite stood up and proclaimed, "**Let the contest begin!**"

A CONTEST TO THE LAST SPOONFUL!

The dishes began to arrive at the judges' table. Each one was served by a sprite who was smiling and hoping to make a good impression.

"It won't be easy to pick a winner," Helios remarked.

"You're right. I have no idea how to choose," Paulina agreed. "I'm just happy we get to eat twenty dishes."

Just then, a sprite placed a **steaming** plate in front of the judges. "Here are my fried flowers stuffed with caramelized dew," he said. "They'll leave you speechless! They were prepared following a **very old**

recipe. The batter is made with **pink** potato flour and the dew must be collected during the moment before dawn."

"It sounds like a very **complicated** recipe," Princess Flora observed.

"It's not a dish that just any chef could prepare," the sprite said with a smug **smile**.

"Well, we'll have to **taste** it," said Helios, taking the first bite. "It's very good. Well done!"

"**Yes, delicious**," added Paulina.

It's a very elaborate recipe!

The sprite stepped back, satisfied.

More dishes, each more elaborate, followed. Each of the sprites described the **ingredients** and the method of preparation very carefully, to show how difficult

the dishes were to make.

The Thea Sisters, the princess, and Helios listened carefully to the **technical explanations** before tasting.

"They're all so different and complicated," Colette remarked.

"Sometimes it's even difficult to recognize which **ingredients** have been used," added Pamela.

It was the last sprite's turn. He approached the table with some **uncertainty** and placed his dish right in front of Princess Flora.

"This is my dish," he said with a **BOW**. "**MUSHROOM**

SOUP," Nicky commented, a bit surprised.

"Nothing complicated," added Princess Flora. "A simple dish, but made with care."

"It's a **recipe** I learned from my mother, who learned it from her mother," he explained shyly. "They weren't sophisticated cooks, but they always cooked with **love**."

"Let's taste it," Helios said.

Pam took a spoonful of soup. "This is even **better** than pizza!"

The others also tried the **SOUP** the sprite had made.

He remained a little ways off, his eyes low, waiting to be **judged**.

All twenty dishes had been tasted. The judges put their heads together for a discussion. After a few minutes, Princess Flora declared, "We have a decision."

"Well, Princess, what is the winning dish?" the Great Sprite asked.

The princess turned to the contestants. "Thank you for letting us taste all these wonderful dishes. After consulting with one another, the dish that we feel deserves to win is . . . the WILD MUSHROOM SOUP!" she announced.

A loud murmuring broke out from the sprites.

Thank you!

"Silence!" the Great Sprite ordered. He looked at the princess. "Can you explain the reason for your choice?"

"This soup was the most delicious thing we tasted, but

above all, it was made with **much love**," the princess replied.

The Great Sprite looked pleased. "Thank you, Princess. Today we have learned something very important from you," he said. "Now tell me what you need and I will fulfill your request, as promised."

"We need to get to the **TOWER OF THE DARK TULIP**," Princess Flora said. "Can you show us the way?"

His eyes widened. "Do you really want to go to such a terrifying place? It's full of **evil magic**!"

"We know that, but we have no choice," Helios said.

The sprite was silent for a moment. "Very well," he said finally. "I will go with you. Quickly, let's get moving, before **DARKNESS** falls."

THE SECRET CORRIDOR

The Great Sprite and a small group of Green Sprites led them through the forest. As they got closer to the Tower of the Dark Tulip, a creepy feeling came over everyone.

They emerged from the trees onto barren, ROCKY ground. The tower jutted out in front of them, GHOSTLY, threatening, and forbidding, protected by a stone wall.

"It's VERY HIGH," Nicky observed.

"And very dark," added Violet.

"How do we get through the wall?" asked Colette.

"There's an entrance behind that WATERFALL," explained the Great Sprite,

pointing to a spot in front of them.

Another sprite spoke up. "Once you enter, a long, dark tunnel will lead you to the inside of the tower. It's full of **TRAPS**, but it's the only way."

"When you're inside the tunnel, you must **count** your steps according to the rules of the tower," the Great Sprite explained.

"What do you mean?" asked Paulina. "Is there some kind of pattern to follow?"

"You must step on **twelve** stones, and then skip over the **thirteenth** stone," the sprite replied. "Then count twelve stones again, and skip over the thirteenth, until you reach the tower door."

"What happens if we **STEP** on the thirteenth stone?" Colette asked.

"If you make a mistake, the ground will open up beneath you and you'll end up in the

The tower!
How do we get in?

The entrance is behind the waterfall!

River of Despair," the sprite replied.

"That doesn't sound like fun," Pam remarked.

"It is not," the sprite said. "The River of Despair is an underground stream that flows into the **DARK GORGE**, the darkest and most inhospitable place in the kingdom."

The princess turned to the sprites. "Thank you so much for bringing us here."

"It was a pleasure to help you, Your Highness," the **Great Sprite** replied. Then he and the other sprites headed back to the village.

Helios started for the **WATERFALL**. "Come on, I'll go first," he said.

The Thea Sisters and Princess Flora followed him.

"**Brrr! It's so icy!**" Colette said.

Up ahead, they heard Helios call out, "I

found the opening of the corridor to the tower!"

They caught up to him and peered into the dark, narrow **tunnel**.

"It's so dark in there," Colette observed.

"We must go forward very **carefully**, relying on our other senses, not our sight," the princess remarked.

"Walk behind me and remember the **rule of the steps**," Helios said.

"We will!" the Thea Sisters promised, but they were all feeling uncertain and **scared**.

They stepped inside the tunnel.

"Holy hubcaps! It's as dark as a **CHEESE CAVE** in here," Pam remarked.

"This darkness is darker than dark . . ." Colette whispered.

"Stick close to one another," Helios suggested. "And remember to count."

They whispered to themselves as they walked.

"One step . . . two steps . . . four steps . . . eight steps . . ."

Suddenly, Violet called out. "I LOST COUNT of my steps!"

"Think back, Vi," said Paulina. "You're behind me, and I just took my twelfth step, I'm sure. And you're three stones behind me. Catch up to me, and we'll jump together."

"Okay," Violet said. She took three **careful** steps until she reached Paulina.

"All right," she said. "We're going to JUMP. Don't worry, I won't let you fall into the River of Despair."

The two friends jumped over the thirteenth stone.

"We'll move on together," Paulina said. "Let's start counting. One . . . two . . . three . . ."

The sound of everyone counting at the same time echoed throughout the tunnel.

"I feel something in front of me," Helios called back to the others. "It's solid. It could be a WALL or a door."

Colette stopped. "Great! I'll be right . . ."

Her voice trailed off. "I can't remember if I've gone eleven steps or twelve," she said. Everyone counting at the same time had confused her. "I'm pretty sure it's eleven, though. It's got to be."

"Twelve!" Colette said confidently, stepping on the stone in front of her.

Suddenly, the walls began to **CREAK** and the stones beneath them started to crumble.

The Thea Sisters grabbed paws and ran, with Princess Flora *flying* beside them. They reached the rock ledge in front of the door just as the rest of the path **crumbled** behind them and fell into the River of Despair.

Trembling, they turned to the entrance: a **DOOR** with a large iron ring for a handle.

They had reached the

TOWER OF THE DARK TULIP.

This must be the entrance!

THE TOWER OF THE DARK TULIP

The Thea Sisters, Princess Flora, and Helios squeezed onto the narrow **ROCK LEDGE**. They tried to push open the large **DOOR**, but it wouldn't budge.

"Did you try turning the ring?" Colette asked Nicky.

"Yes, in all directions, but nothing happened," Nicky replied.

"This door is **SO HEAVY**," said Violet. "We'll never be able to move it on our own."

"I'm afraid that it's the only way we can enter the tower," the knight explained.

"We've got to figure out how to OPEN it," Pamela concluded.

"And we have to do it **quickly**!" Paulina

added. "This rock ledge is trembling under my feet."

Paulina studied the door. "Maybe there's a hidden inscription that tells how to open it."

"Or maybe you need to say magic words to open it," Pam suggested.

"I have an idea," the princess said. "Let me try."

Then she closed her eyes, took a **deep breath**, and walked confidently toward the door. Then, to everyone's amazement, she passed right through it!

"No way!" Pam cried. "What just happened?"

Princess Flora

appeared once again, coming through the door.

"The door is just an illusion created by magic," she explained. "All you have to do is close your eyes. Then walk straight ahead, believing that the door doesn't exist. If you do, you'll pass right through it!"

"I'll TRY it!" Colette replied. She closed her eyes and took a few steps forward. Then disappeared through the heavy door.

"I did it!" she cried from the other side.

One by one, the others passed through the door until they were all inside the tower. They had entered a large empty entrance hall, filled with an icy cold light. A winding staircase of dark stone rose up in front of them.

"That's got more twists than string cheese," Pam remarked.

Colette looked up to the top of the staircase. "I can't see where it ends! It looks like it goes on **forever**!

"It could be an **illusion**," Helios told her. "This tower is full of **TRICKS** to discourage intruders."

"My **sister** may be at the top of this staircase. I must go up," Princess Flora said, taking the first step.

Pam looked at her friends. "Guess we're heading up this spooky staircase!"

The five friends started to climb the tower staircase, not knowing where it would lead them.

"I hope this staircase isn't just another magical illusion, like the door," Colette remarked.

They climbed and climbed, until finally they found themselves in a large hall with a HIGH ceiling, supported by columns. A bluish light filtered through the room, which was ghostly silent.

"Look, there's another staircase leading to the top floor," Princess Flora said, pointing.

"Well, actually there are two more," added Nicky. "No, wait, three. No . . . four!"

Everyone watched, speechless, as staircases appeared all over the room. Some led up and

some led down. They kept changing direction, and disappeared and reappeared all around the hall.

"This looks like WITCHY magic to me," Colette said with a frown.

"How exactly are we supposed to figure this out?" Pam asked. "It's not like we can fight MAGIC with magic."

"The power of our friendship is magical," Violet said. "If we stick together, we'll defeat this witch."

Helios nodded. "We must be strong," he said. "Let's follow one staircase and see where it leads us."

The the team bravely stepped down the nearest magical staircase . . .

Let's stay together!

Should we try this one?

THE EYES OF THE HEART

They walked **UP** the stairs and **DOWN** the stairs, trying to keep up with the stone steps as they moved. Violet took a step just as the staircase in front of her disappeared, but Colette was there to grab her paw before she fell.

Violet was shaken, but she still smiled. "See? The magic of friendship saved me!"

Finally, they reached a landing made of **smooth** stone. The staircases all vanished.

"**We made it!**" Pam cheered.

"And now we have to find my sister," said Princess Flora, her eyes shining with hope.

They looked around the circular landing. There were **CLOSED** doors along the wall, all

around the circle.

"Farrah could be **behind** one of these doors," Helios said. He tugged on the nearest one, but it wouldn't open.

"This one won't OPEN, either!" Colette announced.

"Nor this one!" Princess Flora added.

"Before we keep trying, we should try to figure out if **PRINCESS FARRAH** is even behind one of these doors," Violet said.

Colette nodded. "Let's try calling to her," Colette suggested.

"Farrah, where are you? Sister, it's me! Open up, please!" shouted Princess Flora.

Nothing happened.

"Farrah! It's me!" Princess Flora shouted again.

Princess Flora frowned. "I am doing this all wrong," she said. She closed her eyes. Everyone was quiet. Then she opened them and walked directly to one of the doors.

She reached out and placed her hands on the **HEAVY DOOR** in front of her.

"Farrah is behind this door," she said.

"Are you SURE?" Helios asked.

"Yes, Helios," she replied. "Ever since we were little, my sister and I could feel each

other's presence. I don't know how to explain it, but you must believe me."

Helios grabbed the doorknob and tried to open the door. Unbelievably, the hinges **GROANED** and the door opened without any resistance.

"**FARRAH!**" Princess Flora cried, and she ran into the room.

Her twin was seated on a large armchair and her eyes were staring **blankly** into space, as if she didn't see her sister or the others.

Princess Flora ran to her and knelt in front of her.

"*My sister!*" she cried.

But her twin didn't move.

"Don't you recognize me?" Flora asked.

"She is probably the **VICTIM** of some enchantment," Helios guessed.

"You're right," Princess Flora said with a

sigh. She looked at her sister. "She seems so different."

"What do you mean?" Paulina asked.

"Farrah's eyes always shone with **warmth** and happiness," the princess explained. "But now, they are dull and EMPTY."

Her eyes full of tears, Princess Flora tried to hug her sister. But Princess Farrah did not return her embrace. She pushed Flora away sharply, as if she were afraid.

Princess Flora looked at her in surprise.

"Farrah, I am your sister. We must return to the ***Golden Dahlia Palace***. It is our home. Do you remember?" she asked.

"No, I will never **go back** to that place," Princess Farrah replied. Her words sounded as if they were coming from a **DARK**, far-off universe.

Helios knelt before her. "Princess Farrah, I am Helios. Do you remember me? I saved you from the Lilies of False Memory, and returned with you to the palace."

She turned to him with an EMPTY look. "I don't know you."

At that exact moment, an ICY whirlwind swept into the room. As soon as the gray fog cleared, a hooded figure appeared, holding a staff topped with a dark tulip. She spoke in a thundering voice.

"Stop where you are! You're not taking her anywhere!"

"THE WITCH!" Helios cried.

The witch cackled in a hoarse, grating voice. "Ha, ha, ha! You have no magic to use against me. What do you think you're going to do?"

"We are going to bring my sister, Farrah,

The witch!
Stop right there!

back home!" replied Princess Flora. "I'm not afraid of you, Amarantha!"

"FARRAH is now MINE. And I will keep her prisoner until I no longer need her," Amarantha said.

Just then, Paulina noticed that the witch was clutching something in her wrinkled hand. "Those are the roses from the Timeless Rose Garden!" she cried.

"You took them!" shouted Princess Flora, her eyes filling with tears. "I was sure that my sister would never have done such a thing of her own free will!"

"And she is not done doing my bidding yet," Amarantha said. "After she collects three more Mother Roses for me, I will complete the Absolute Elixir. It is not yet powerful enough for my needs." She grasped the vial hanging around her neck. "Once it is

complete, I will force you to leave your throne, and I shall become **QUEEN OF THE FLOWERS**!" she shrieked, bursting into cruel laughter.

THE DUEL WITH THE WITCH

"NO ONE CAN STOP ME NOW!" Amarantha cried.

"That's what you think!" Helios replied, launching himself at her.

The witch, taken by surprise, let the roses fall to the ground and hurled a ball of fire at the knight. He skillfully dodged it.

"The roses!" Colette yelled, and she rushed to pick them up.

"How dare you?" the witch shrieked. She raised a hand and aimed another fireball at Colette.

Nicky quickly grabbed Colette by the wrist and pulled her to the ground, saving her from the fiery sphere.

Colette looked dazed. "Thanks, Nicky!" Then she quickly picked up the fallen roses.

"Quick, let's get out of here," her friend replied.

"**YOU WON'T GET AWAY!**" the witch screamed.

Just then, Princess Flora realized something. Amarantha had not used her **staff** against them but had kept it pointed at Farrah.

The princess whispered to the others, "The witch is controlling my sister with the staff. I think it keeps her from awakening from the enchantment and coming with us."

"Then we must find a way to get the scepter away from the witch," Helios said.

"I've got an idea," Paulina said, and she whispered her plan to the others.

Princess Flora nodded. "That could work!"

WHOOSH! The witch hurled a ball of

flame right at Paulina! She dodged it just in time, but it hit one of the curtains over the window, setting it aflame.

"**YOU'LL BE SORRY YOU EVER FOUGHT AGAINST ME!**" Amarantha shouted, and she raised her hand, ready to attack again.

Paulina and Pam ran away from the others.

"Over here! You can't **CATCH** us!" they taunted her.

"Oh, I can't?" the witch cried. She turned to follow them. But while her back was turned, Princess Flora **grabbed** the staff right from her hand!

Princess Farrah blinked her eyes.

"Flora, my sister," she cried as her eyes filled with **LIGHT** again. "You're here!"

"Farrah! You're you again!" her sister cried, smiling.

Amarantha held out her right hand, and the staff returned to her.

"**NO!**" she yelled. "**I WILL NOT PERMIT YOU TO RUIN MY PLAN!**"

Helios charged her once more. Her eyes filled with rage and then blue light flew from her staff, creating a **fiery barrier** that imprisoned the knight.

The witch cackled and pointed the staff at the princess once more. Dark blue light snaked out. Before the magic could hit Princess Farrah, Princess Flora JUMPED in front of it. She blocked her sister with her own body!

"You shall not take my sister again!" Princess Flora cried. She closed her eyes,

waiting for the evil magic to hit her.

But the magical blast did not strike Princess Flora. Instead, it completely vanished! The Thea Sisters looked on, **amazed**, as the fiery barrier around Helios disappeared, too.

"What just happened?" Paulina asked.

"It is the power of **true love**," Helios replied. "The love between the two sisters was more powerful than any of this witch's magic."

Violet smiled. "I knew there was something more **powerful** than her magic."

Helios nodded.

"Yes. And now all of Amarantha's **TRICKS** and **TRAPS** in the castle will fade as well."

Suddenly, Princess Farrah jumped to her feet. She **BRAVELY** ran to the witch and yanked on the vial of **Absolute Elixir** that was hanging around the witch's neck. It broke off the cord and fell into the princess's hand.

"**NOOO! GIVE THAT BACK!**" Amarantha shouted, pointing the staff at her. But she had lost all her power.

No more magic glowed from the **dark tulip** on the end of the staff.

"Your power is gone, witch!" Princess Farrah said.

Amarantha glared at the princess. "**YOU'LL PAY FOR THIS!**" she threatened one last time, and then she vanished in a swirl of ashes.

Then the tower began to shake from its very foundations.

"Everything's going to collapse! We must get out of here!" Helios shouted.

Luckily, without the witch's magic, an ordinary staircase led them down from the tower. They reached the bottom quickly.

"Let's get as far away as possible!" Princess Flora shouted.

They were just in time, because the terrifying Tower of the Dark Tulip **collapsed** in ruins behind them. A cloud of **dust** rose up from the rubble.

Everyone **STOPPED** a moment to catch their breath. They turned to look at the ruined tower. The dark clouds overhead were parting, and **sunlight** streamed down. Princess Flora held hands with her sister and Helios, and the Thea Sisters linked paws.

As the **sun** hit the hill on which the tower sat, **green** grass appeared. Then tiny sprouts. They watched, amazed, as the **sprouts** grew before their eyes, transforming into beautiful **red tulips**.

Look!
Tulips!

A FLORAL SYMPHONY

Colette clutched the precious **roses**. "Now we can go back to the Timeless Rose Garden and save the kingdom," she said.

"I just hope that Will and Yarrow are okay, and the palace is safe," Paulina said.

"I'm sure everything's fine," Nicky assured her. "Will is an **EXPERT** agent."

"The **sooner** we get back to the palace, the **sooner** we'll save the kingdom," Helios pointed out.

"If you agree, perhaps we could pass through the village of **Happy Blossom**," Princess Farrah

suggested, watching Princess Flora consult the Crystal Compass.

"That sounds like a much friendlier place than the Tower of the Dark Tulip," Pam remarked.

"What kind of village is it?" Colette asked.

"It's where the Perfume Fairies live," Princess Farrah explained. "And it's quite a lovely place. It's on the way. Let's go!"

Everyone followed the princess, who looked beautiful and happy now that she was out from under the witch's spell. They crossed a field of pink daisies, then a field of BLUE IRISES, and at last a field of white lilies. In some places, the flowers had wilted or the blossoms had stopped blooming.

"Once we replant the Mother Roses in the Timeless Rose Garden, I'm sure these

Let's go!

flowers will be healthy again," Violet said hopefully.

"Yarrow will know what to do," Princess Flora assured her.

"The village is just over that brook, right?" asked Helio. "I visited it once with my comrades from the Order of the Sunflower."

The princess nodded, and then turned to the Thea Sisters. "The Perfume Fairies who live in Happy Blossom are the most skilled perfume makers in the kingdom. They create unique, personalized scents that adapt perfectly to whoever wears them."

Colette clapped her paws together. "This sounds amazing. I've always wanted to learn how to make perfumes."

"How do we cross to the other side?" Paulina wondered.

Nicky grinned. "One step at a time," she replied.

She leaped onto one of the STONES that jutted out of the water. Then, careful not to lose her balance, she jumped from stone to stone until she reached the other side.

"**FUN!**" said Pam, and she did the same, taking a different route.

The other Thea Sisters crossed the brook. Princess Flora **FLEW** over. But Princess Farrah was still too weak to fly.

"Let me **HELP** you, Princess," Helios said to her.

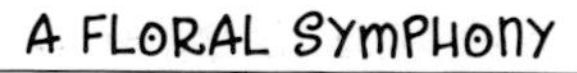

He took Princess Farrah's hand and they crossed the brook together SLOWLY, stone by stone. The princess looked at the knight and GAZED into his eyes.

"Look at those two," Colette whispered to her friends. "So romantic!"

They all continued on to Happy Blossom, which was bordered by a hedge of LAVENDER bushes. They stepped through the border into a VILLAGE containing wooden houses with roofs made of flower petals. Colorful ribbons adorned the windows and doors of each home.

"What a charming place!" Colette remarked.

"I would love to live in a place like this," said Violet.

As they walked toward the COLORFUL homes, one fairy came out to greet them.

"Welcome to **Happy Blossom**!" she said, and then her eyes got wide as she recognized the princesses. "Your Highnesses! What an HONOR to have you here with us." She smiled at them and bowed deeply.

"Kind *Perfume Fairy*, our friends would like to try the perfumed essences for which you are so famous," Princess Flora replied.

"Of course!" the fairy said.

"This is our **laboratory**, where we prepare all of the essences," the fairy explained, while around her the workers bowed as the princesses passed.

The Thea Sisters admired the fairies' work and listened as the fairies described how

they mixed **flower essences** to make different kinds of perfumes.

"This is Floral Symphony, one of our latest creations," one fairy explained, handing

the Thea Sisters a **glass bottle** the color of apricots.

Colette removed the top and sniffed. "It's wonderful!"

The fairies let them smell many more of their perfumes. The Thea Sisters could have stayed there all day, but they politely thanked the fairies and set out again with the princesses and Helios.

Their **MISSION** wasn't over yet!

RETURN TO THE LAND OF FLOWERS

As soon as they glimpsed the sparkling petals of the Golden Dahlia Palace in the distance, the two faces of the two princesses lit up with happiness.

Princess Flora entered first, followed by Princess Farrah. The returning princess looked around with shining eyes, as if it were the first time she had stepped foot there.

"It seems as if I were away for a very long time," she said.

"But you're home now, dear sister," Princess Flora said. "And I couldn't be happier."

A few of the Summer Flower Fairies ran to

meet them and gathered around Princess Farrah.

"What a joy to have you back, Your Highness!"

The fairies all began dancing and singing to

celebrate Princess Farrah's return. Will and Yarrow soon joined them. "**Thea Sisters, I am so happy to see you!**" Will exclaimed.

The Thea Sisters **reported** everything

that had happened since they had left the **palace**, trying not to leave out any details.

"I knew you could do it," Will said proudly.

"We would **never** let the Seven Roses Unit down," Pam assured him.

Princess Flora approached the group with her sister. "Will, do you remember Princess **FARRAH**?" she asked.

Will bowed. "It's good to see you home again, Your Highness," he said.

"It's thanks to your **partners**," Princess Farrah said, smiling at the Thea Sisters.

Yarrow looked at the mouselets, amazed. "You defeated the witch, got the **Absolute Elixir** from her, and took down the tower?" he asked in disbelief.

"We did more than that," Colette replied with a smile. "We brought back the stolen **Mother Roses**. They are losing their color,

but I am sure that you know how to take care of them." She handed them to him.

"Thank you so much," he replied. "I will replant them in the Timeless Rose Garden. Come and see."

They all followed him to the **Timeless Rose Garden**. When they arrived at the bed of the **Mother Roses**, Yarrow knelt down and put the roses on the ground. With a spade, he dug **three little holes** in the soft, fragrant soil.

Then, with great care, he took the first rose and put the stem and roots in the soil. He refilled the hole and patted down the soil to make sure the **flower** was well planted. He repeated the same process with the other roses.

"Now can you pass me the **Absolute Elixir**, please?" he asked.

Princess Farrah handed him the **precious essence**, and he placed a few drops on the **petals** of the replanted roses, and on the ground around them.

For a moment, nothing happened. Then, little by little, the pale, wilted petals started to regain their **COLOR** and **freshness** and, splendid once more, raised themselves up strong and shining in the **sunlight**.

Yarrow smiled at everyone's shocked

looks and explained, "The **Absolute Elixir** contains the pure essential energy of the Mother Roses. I've used it to give them back their **strength** and **beauty**."

"Look," Princess Farrah added, motioning all around her. "The **Timeless Rose Garden** is sparkling!

"I think that we should **celebrate**," Princess Flora said. "What do you think, sister?"

"Of course!" her sister replied, smiling.

"**Wonderful**! Let's organize a Grand Flower Ball, more festive than the kingdom has ever seen!" Princess Flora announced.

At that, everyone cried,

"HOORAY!"

And the grand preparations began.

THE GRAND FLOWER BALL

The Thea Sisters and Will remained in the palace until the day of the Grand Flower Ball. When that day finally arrived, Golden Dahlia Palace was ready. The ORCHESTRA of Blooming Winds traveled across the kingdom for the occasion, and the guests were starting to arrive at the palace.

Colette looked at the invitation. "It's just too bad that we don't have ball gowns for such a fancy affair."

Princess Farrah overheard her. "You mustn't worry about that,"

she said. “Come with me!”

The princess led the Thea Sisters into the ROYAL WARDROBE, filled with beautiful gowns. “Please choose whatever you like! And have fun,” Princess Farrah said. “I’m going to get ready; when you’re dressed, I’ll be waiting for you in the

Dancing Flower Ballroom."

The Thea Sisters thanked the princess and began looking through the dresses. Each one found a DRESS that was absolutely perfect!

They admired their **new looks** in the large wardrobe mirror, and then they went to join the other guests.

"You look just like Flower Fairies," Will remarked as he saw them coming down the palace's grand staircase.

The Fairies of the Four Seasons greeted them with big smiles.

"We'd like to thank you from the bottoms of our hearts for what you did for OUR KINGDOM," one of the Spring Flower Fairies said.

"We are happy to have helped you, dear

fairies," Colette replied on behalf of them all.

The fairies bowed. "We hope you have **FUN** at our party," a Summer Flower Fairy replied, and then they headed for the ballroom.

"Look, the **Dewdrop Fairies** are here!" Violet cried happily.

"And over there I see the Green Sprites!" Pam said. "I wonder if they brought any food with them?"

"And the *Perfume Fairies*!" added Colette.

Just then a group of **new guests** entered the ballroom, and attracted everyone's attention. The handsome young men wore white-and-**BLUE** uniforms.

"Noble **Knights of the Order of the Sunflower**, it is an honor to have you as guests at our

ball," Princess Flora greeted them.

"We thank you for the invitation, Princesses," one of the knights replied.

Then, the **OLDEST** of the knights turned to Helios and shook his hand warmly. "We looked everywhere for you!" he said.

"What's important is that you're

here now, safe and sound. We couldn't be **happier**."

"It's good to be with you again," Helios replied. "I would like you to witness this special moment."

He turned to **PRINCESS FARRAH** and knelt in front of her. "Princess Farrah, will you do me the honor of becoming ***my wife***?" he asked.

The room was silent as everyone waited for her answer. She gave it with a smile. **"YES!"**

"**HOORAY!**" everyone cheered.

"Long live the noble knight Helios and his fiancée, Princess Farrah!" the Knights of the Sunflower shouted.

At the end of the night, the Perfume Fairies approached the Thea Sisters and handed them five **packages** wrapped in rice paper.

Will you marry me?
Yes!

How romantic!
Hooray!

"We would like you to take a small souvenir to remember our kingdom," one of them said.

"They're **five essences** created especially for each of you," another explained.

"This is an **incredible** gift!" Paulina added.

THE SECRET PASSAGE

The next morning, it was time for the Thea Sisters to go back to **MOUSEFORD**.

The two princesses gave them a **warm** farewell.

"Thank you so much for saving our kingdom," Princess Flora said.

"And thank you for bringing me home," added Princess Farrah.

"We're glad we could help," Colette said.

"We're sorry that you have to go so soon," Princess Flora continued. "Can we arrange for fairies to accompany you partway?"

"That would be very helpful, thanks!" said Will.

"Then farewell, dear friends," Princess

Flora said. "Get home safely."

"Farewell, Princesses!" the Thea Sisters said.

When they left the palace, a group of Fairies of the Four Seasons were waiting to accompany them in flight.

"When you are ready, we can go," one of them said.

Will and the Thea Sisters turned to take one last look at the sparkling **palace**. Then Will nodded.

"We're ready," he said.

The fairies then took them by the paws and **soared** into the yellow sky.

"It's so exciting

to fly one last time in this WORLD!" Nicky remarked.

"Did you notice how BRIGHT the colors of the flowers are now?" Colette asked.

"Thanks to the Absolute Elixir!" Pam replied.

"And thanks to all of you," Will added.

The Thea Sisters smiled happily.

When they had crossed the plain, the fairies gently lowered them down to the ground. Will and the Thea Sisters thanked them and said good-bye. Then they started looking for the crystal elevator.

"Why can't we find it?" Violet wondered.

Will looked around, confused. "This is **definitely** the spot."

"What could have happened?" asked Pam.

Will looked thoughtful. "I have a theory. Perhaps the Absolute Elixir used on the

Mother Roses has caused every plant in the kingdom to grow more rapidly."

"Then is the crystal elevator buried under the plants?" Violet asked.

"It's possible," Will replied.

They all pushed aside vines and leaves, looking for the elevator that was their ride home. Then Will called out, "I think I found it! But there's a **problem**."

The five friends gasped. The elevator was completely covered by a climbing plant!

"What do we do now?" Pam asked.

"I think I know," Colette said. "When we've visited other fantasy worlds, there has always been a secret passage that leads back to our world."

"That's right, Colette," Will told her.

Paulina's eyes brightened. "And you know where the passage is in the Land of Flowers, Will, because you've used it before!"

"Exactly, Paulina," Will said, smiling at her. "It's hidden behind a ROCK WALL covered by wisteria. It must not be far from here, to the north."

The group started walking, and shortly thereafter, as Will had said, they ran into the rock wall covered in PURPLE flowers.

They searched for the opening through the

thick clusters of flowers with no luck.

"Will, the **VEGETATION** is too thick," Paulina reported. "I can't see anything."

"Me neither," Colette added. "As soon as I move a branch, another one falls in its place."

"You're right," Will agreed. "This isn't working."

Violet spoke up. "In the book my parents sent me from China, I read that wisteria vine has a very **SOLID** trunk," she said. "If it's strong enough, maybe we can **climb** up it and get a better look."

"**I'll do it!**" Nicky offered right away. She located the trunk of the plant and began to climb **carefully** onto the low branches. Her friends watched as she ventured up between the bunches of flowers.

"**There's an opening here!**" she cried a moment later.

"Sometimes you just need to change your point of view in order to find the solution to a problem," Will said.

"That's very true!" the others agreed.

Then one by one they hoisted themselves up into the **wisteria** and went through the secret passage beyond the flowering wall.

There's a passageway here!

On the other side, the helicopter of the Seven Roses Unit was already ready to **depart**.

SPRING FESTIVAL AT MOUSEFORD

Once they were back at Mouseford, the Thea Sisters threw themselves back into planning the Spring Festival.

"What a shame that Thea wasn't able to come," Violet said with a sigh as they were finishing decorations one day.

A few hours later, the five friends received a message on their **cell phones**:

> Thea Sisters, I am very proud of you, and so is Will. You make a great team, even without us. I hope to see you soon. Yours, Thea.

"I know Thea will be with us tomorrow in

spirit," Colette said.

Paulina yawned. "We should get some sleep. Tomorrow will be a long day!"

The morning of the Spring Festival dawned bright and sunny. Colette woke up early to do her hair. As she got ready, she glanced at the bracelet on her wrist: It was the bracelet with the Sweet Memory Flower that Princess Flora had given her.

"This is a beautiful bracelet," she told Pam. "But I will never **forget** the Land of Flowers, no matter what!"

"Neither will I," Pam agreed.

Then Paulina appeared in the doorway with Nicky and Violet.

"Come on!" she urged. "We've got lots of new **memories** to make!"

Then the Thea Sisters ran off to enjoy the Spring Festival. When they got there,

Yeah, yeah, yeah!
Hooray for spring!

What a great party!

they couldn't help feeling proud. The decorations, the buffet, the flowers . . . everything was perfect!

Then Nicky's eyes got WIDE. "Hey, did anyone else see that? That bush just moved!"

"It was only the *wind* . . ." Pam replied.

". . . or maybe a Flower Fairy!" Colette added with a big smile.

Don't miss any of my fabumouse special editions!

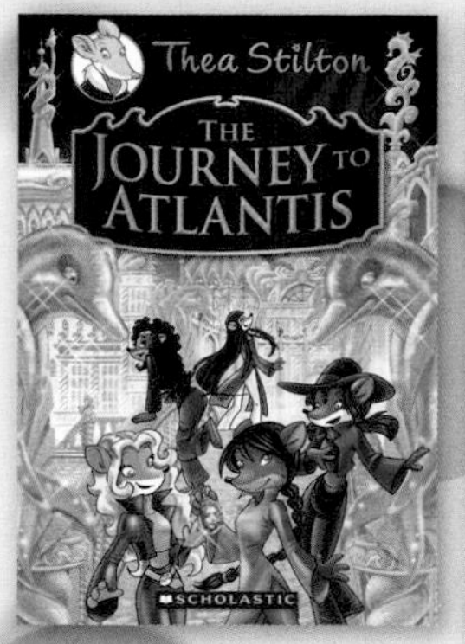

THE JOURNEY TO ATLANTIS

THE SECRET OF THE FAIRIES

THE SECRET OF THE SNOW

THE CLOUD CASTLE

THE TREASURE OF THE SEA

THE LAND OF FLOWERS

Don't miss any of these exciting Thea Sisters adventures!

Thea Stilton and the Dragon's Code

Thea Stilton and the Mountain of Fire

Thea Stilton and the Ghost of the Shipwreck

Thea Stilton and the Secret City

Thea Stilton and the Mystery in Paris

Thea Stilton and the Cherry Blossom Adventure

Thea Stilton and the Star Castaways

Thea Stilton: Big Trouble in the Big Apple

Thea Stilton and the Ice Treasure

Thea Stilton and the Secret of the Old Castle

Thea Stilton and the Blue Scarab Hunt

Thea Stilton and the Prince's Emerald

Thea Stilton and the Mystery on the Orient Express

Thea Stilton and the Dancing Shadows

Thea Stilton and the Legend of the Fire Flowers

Thea Stilton and the Spanish Dance Mission

Thea Stilton and the Journey to the Lion's Den

Thea Stilton and the Great Tulip Heist

Thea Stilton and the Chocolate Sabotage

Thea Stilton and the Missing Myth

Thea Stilton and the Lost Letters

Thea Stilton and the Tropical Treasure

Thea Stilton and the Hollywood Hoax

Thea Stilton and the Madagascar Madness

Thea Stilton and the Frozen Fiasco

Thea Stilton and the Venice Masquerade

Be sure to read all my fabumouse adventures!

#1 Lost Treasure of the Emerald Eye

#2 The Curse of the Cheese Pyramid

#3 Cat and Mouse in a Haunted House

#4 I'm Too Fond of My Fur!

#5 Four Mice Deep in the Jungle

#6 Paws Off, Cheddarface!

#7 Red Pizzas for a Blue Count

#8 Attack of the Bandit Cats

#9 A Fabumouse Vacation for Geronimo

#10 All Because of a Cup of Coffee

#11 It's Halloween, You 'Fraidy Mouse!

#12 Merry Christmas, Geronimo!

#13 The Phantom of the Subway

#14 The Temple of the Ruby of Fire

#15 The Mona Mousa Code

#16 A Cheese-Colored Camper

#17 Watch Your Whiskers, Stilton!

#18 Shipwreck on the Pirate Islands

#19 My Name Is Stilton, Geronimo Stilton

#20 Surf's Up, Geronimo!

#21 The Wild, Wild West

#22 The Secret of Cacklefur Castle

A Christmas Tale

#23 Valentine's Day Disaster

#24 Field Trip to Niagara Falls

#25 The Search for Sunken Treasure

#26 The Mummy with No Name

#27 The Christmas Toy Factory

#28 Wedding Crasher

#29 Down and Out Down Under

#30 The Mouse Island Marathon

#31 The Mysterious Cheese Thief

Christmas Catastrophe

#32 Valley of the Giant Skeletons

#33 Geronimo and the Gold Medal Mystery

#34 Geronimo Stilton, Secret Agent

#35 A Very Merry Christmas

#36 Geronimo's Valentine

#37 The Race Across America

#38 A Fabumouse School Adventure

#39 Singing Sensation

#40 The Karate Mouse

#41 Mighty Mount Kilimanjaro

#42 The Peculiar Pumpkin Thief

#43 I'm Not a Supermouse!

#44 The Giant Diamond Robbery

#45 Save the White Whale!

#46 The Haunted Castle

#47 Run for the Hills, Geronimo!

#48 The Mystery in Venice

#49 The Way of the Samurai

#50 This Hotel Is Haunted!

#51 The Enormouse Pearl Heist

#52 Mouse in Space!

#53 Rumble in the Jungle

#54 Get into Gear, Stilton!

#55 The Golden Statue Plot

#56 Flight of the Red Bandit

The Hunt for the Golden Book

#57 The Stinky Cheese Vacation

#58 The Super Chef Contest

#59 Welcome to Moldy Manor

The Hunt for the Curious Cheese

#60 The Treasure of Easter Island

#61 Mouse House Hunter

#62 Mouse Overboard!

The Hunt for the Secret Papyrus

#63 The Cheese Experiment

#64 Magical Mission

#65 Bollywood Burglary

The Hunt for the Hundredth Key

#66 Operation: Secret Recipe

#67 The Chocolate Chase